# You Have
# 24 Hours to
# Love Us

by

## Guy Ware

*For Sophy*

*and for Frank and Rebecca*

First published in Great Britain in 2012 by Comma Press
www.commapress.co.uk

'Weathering' was first published in www.pygmygiant.com, Jan 2010.
Earlier versions of the several stories originally appeared as follows:
'Witness Protection' in *Brace*, edited by Jim Hinks (Comma, 2006),
'Cities from a Train' in *Tales of the Decongested* Vol 1; edited by Rebekah Lattin-Rawstrone and Paul Blaney (Apis Books, 2006),
'All Downhill from Here' in *London Magazine*, Aug/Sept 2009,
'Aria with Different Variations' in *Litro* No.43, Feb 2007.

A CIP catalogue record of this book is available from the British Library.

ISBN  1905583265
ISBN-13  978 1905583263

The publisher gratefully acknowledges the assistance of Arts Council England, and the support of Literature Northwest.

**LOTTERY FUNDED**

Set in Bembo 11/13 by David Eckersall
Printed and bound in England by MPG Biddles Ltd.

# Contents

# Witness Protection

THE HOUSE HE wanted had a shallow porch. He found it at the end of a cul-de-sac, part of a new estate grafted onto the village. The houses were all built of faded yellow brick. They were not identical and did not face in the same direction. But, all the same, they pressed too hard against an acid green field of winter wheat: the edges were too square, the fences too sharp to pass as new. No one could suppose that these houses had not been built together in the same, new century. It was perfect for his purposes. Nobody here would have roots that had not been recently severed.

The outer door was open and he stepped inside, out of a light rain. A waxed cotton coat, still damp, hung from a peg above a pair of small, muddy boots. She could not have been back long herself. Odd, he thought: he would have expected her to be waiting. Surely they had told her it would be today? There were two glass panels in the inner door, but the glass was mottled and he could see nothing through it but dark shadows. There did not appear to be a bell. He knocked on the glass.

A woman opened the door. She was about his age, or slightly younger, perhaps; slight – skinny, even – with a wide face and pale skin. Her dark hair was pulled back from her ears and forehead; a few strands had worked themselves free and gathered in a loose, airy tangle at her temple. She was wearing jeans and a cap-sleeve shirt that showed her upper arms and seemed, in a woman of her age, defiant. The muscles of her arms were smooth. She looked strong, he thought, tempered. Not particularly attractive.

Ah, well, he thought. You tell yourself not to expect too much, but you can't help it. After what they'd said about her, he'd had his hopes.

1

She said, 'You're wet.'

'I told them not to bother bringing me right to the door. Only have to turn the ambulance round to get back out.'

There was a piano in the living room, with a row of framed photographs along the top. The piano itself was plain, unadorned – a functional box, not an item of furniture. On the rack, there was an open score: scrofulous gothic blots, slashing lines and elongated arrowheads scarred the creamy paper.

He said, 'Do you play?'

She handed him a mug of tea, made sure he had hold of it, before answering. '*You* do, remember?'

'Of course.' Of course he did. He had only been here – been *home,* he should start saying – an hour. Already he was allowing himself to relax, to lose his grip on the brief.

He stood, put the mug down carefully, and walked over to the piano. He picked up the score. Schubert. He flipped through the pages. Christ, he thought. I can't do that.

Then: Of course I can't. Guy had been ill. *I've* been ill. That was their point.

In the hour since he'd arrived, Stella – it was time he brought himself to use her name – had asked if he would like a cup of tea, had shown him to the room he would be sleeping in, and had left him to wash and change. He had no clothes of his own, other than those he had on. Guy must have used this spare room for dressing. The wardrobe was full. He chose a pair of cord trousers and a blue and white striped shirt. He found socks and old, well-polished brogues. He stepped back to look at himself, at Guy, in the mirror on the back of the wardrobe door. The clothes were good – old and soft – but all a little too large. He had been ill, he told himself; he had lost weight. He put on an extra pair of socks; the shoes would be all right.

The shirt cuffs hung loose around his wrists: they would need links. There was a leather case on a shelf in the wardrobe. In it, each nestled in its appropriate velvet depression, he found a pair of hairbrushes – leather backed with silver bands – two pairs of nail scissors of different size and a tortoiseshell comb. The bristles on the brushes were soft. There was a small compartment with a lid that he lifted to reveal an assortment of cufflinks, tie clips and a pair of elasticated metal bands that he thought might have been used to hold shirtsleeves in place. He slipped them on, and the slight constriction around his biceps made him feel as if he were donning armour. He chose a pair of cufflinks: small, flat gold ovals linked by thin chains. Each was engraved with a crest he recognised. Guy had been an Old Wellingburian ('75-'80 Parker House): he had been there when there were still boarders; he was there, in the lower sixth, when the first girls arrived. The cufflinks were too small to reproduce the school's bracing motto, *Salus in Arduis,* which, in this mealy-mouthed age, it now preferred to translate as 'Fulfilment through challenge'. All this he knew, or remembered, or had been told.

When he came downstairs, Stella laughed. She said the armbands made him look like an Edwardian bank clerk, and he took them off. She said they were his father's: didn't he remember? So were the cufflinks.

Guy's father had been an Old Wellingburian ('28-'38 Platts), too, he recalled: at least he had died before his son.

She said, 'Would you like to play something now? It might help.'

'Wouldn't it disturb you?'

'Oh, you know me.' Her voice sounded fragile.

He nodded. 'Of course.' He wondered for a moment if he should wink, if she would appreciate it. No. This was a part he would have to get used to. Knowingness, irony would have to go; it could get him killed. Her too, perhaps. Stella was doing him the courtesy of playing it straight; it was up to him to respond, to follow the rules.

'I won't, thank you. I'm a little tired.'

He replaced the score, and looked at the photographs: he – Guy, he should say – and Stella, dressed for a wedding,

3

their wedding; Stella with a small boy and a baby; Guy holding the same baby; Guy with Jason and Annabelle, both in their prep school burgundy blazers; Jason outside the Parker-Steyne's House building in the blue uniform of the Senior School. (They had been two houses in Guy's day.) They'd done a good job with the photographs, he had to give them that. You couldn't see the joins.

Stella said, 'Of course. Have you eaten?'

Dinner was no more uncomfortable than any blind date. They both wanted the evening to pass without difficulty. He praised the food, comparing it favourably to that in the hospital. She laughed and said she should hope so. Her laugh came out surprisingly deep, he thought, for someone of such slight build. She had changed into a blouse through which he could occasionally see the outlines of her bra – which contained nothing much to interest him. She was still wearing the jeans, which had traces of mud around the calves.

'The weather seems to have improved,' he said. 'It was pretty rotten this afternoon.'

'Yes.'

'Had you been out for a walk when I arrived?'

She didn't answer for a while. 'I went to visit the grave.'

'Ah.'

This was awkward, difficult, but how could he change the topic without appearing callous? He had assumed they would have cremated her husband's body, made him disappear in smoke: a grave was always a potential loose end. Still, it wouldn't be the husband's name on the stone – his name now; that much was certain.

'It would have been her birthday.'

It took him a moment to realise how close to a mistake he'd come. She had meant Annabelle, the daughter. Thank Christ for that, he thought. Then: You've got to get a grip on the details, Guy.

'Of course,' he said.

She said there was just fruit for dessert; there might be some ice cream in the freezer. He said an apple would be fine.

After dinner he wanted to go straight to bed; he was tired. Coffee at this time of night would keep him awake, he said, and then make his dreams worse.

He didn't say that he already knew – that he could tell her now if he chose to – exactly what he would dream about. The colours might vary. Some nights they would be heightened, saturated: the blood would look like pillarbox gloss as it pooled on the train floor. On others they were bleached, drained, and the blood would look more like brown sauce as it spread across the floor. Daddies Sauce.

So was it red or brown?

He'd have to say red. It was blood, after all.

They said he should only say things he knew to be true. Anything else would only cause trouble later.

Then they fed him lies.

This you know to be true, they said: your name is Guy West. You are forty-four. Your parents divorced when you were thirteen; you went to Wellingborough School, your father's alma mater. You married Stella West, nee Harris, in 1984. You had two children: Jason and Annabelle. Jason is nineteen and studying Anthropology at Bristol University; Annabelle died four years ago, of leukaemia, at the age of twelve. You were a production manager, initially in the leather goods industry, and later – after the trade collapsed – in light engineering. (Out of the frying pan and into the fire, they allowed themselves to joke: you were not lucky in your choices.) You travelled regularly on business: to India, to Pakistan. When the engineering plant closed as well, you were made redundant. You became depressed and ill. You were treated at St Andrew's Hospital in Northampton. You are now returning home, where you will require a lengthy period of convalescence.

All this you know to be true.

'Good night,' he said. He hesitated, then stepped forward

and kissed her lightly, on the cheek. He felt her watch him climb the stairs.

In the morning, she was brisk.

'How would you like your eggs?'

She had risen before him, showered and dressed. She was wearing jeans again, a clean pair. He was still in his pyjamas.

She made a pot of coffee.

'How are you feeling?' she said. 'Did you dream?'

'Just the usual.'

'What's usual?'

He paused, put down his toast. 'I can't tell you – for your own protection.'

She laughed, and he said: 'I saw someone die.'

'Yes,' she said. 'That's not so unusual.'

He said, 'He was listening to Mahler. That's why I noticed him.'

'Who?'

'The man who died. They didn't like that.'

'You don't kill someone for listening to Mahler.'

He said he meant they didn't believe him.

'I know, Guy.'

She stood behind his chair, then leaned forward and wrapped her arms around him, rested her face on his shoulder. He did not move. He was thinner, harder than the man she knew. She could feel the parts that he was made of.

He had been ill, she thought. He was not yet better.

She persuaded him to walk into the village. She would have to drive into town later, to stock up properly now that he was back, but she needed to pay the paper bill and would buy a few things in the village shop. They were lucky to have it, she said. They should do their bit.

The older houses were low, plump piles of ochreous sandstone. The stone looked soft to Stella, as if she could scratch her name in it with a fingernail, only to see it washed away the next time it rained.

The shop sold newspapers and familiar tinned foods. The owner had recently installed a chilled cabinet and begun to display cheese and meat from local farmers, alongside mozzarella from Italy and sausages from Poland. She was behind the counter when they arrived, cutting chunks of organic Leicester from a wheel and wrapping them in cellophane.

'Morning, Stella. Good morning…' She looked up at Guy and her voice trailed off. 'How are you?'

He said, 'Better, thank you.'

Stella offered the shopkeeper a tight smile. 'He's still not quite himself.'

They left the shop with a tub of olives and a pint of milk. She walked him through the churchyard, where the oldest tombstones had been elbowed into rows to make way for the more recently deceased. She climbed a stile that led onto a muddy footpath beneath wet, bare trees. 'I thought we could go the long way home,' she said. 'Get a breath of air.'

She walked quickly, her shopping bag swinging against her knee, and had to pause from time to time to let him catch up. He had been ill, she told herself, but still. She wanted him to talk again, and she forced herself to slow down.

She had woken during the night and heard his voice. She'd stood at the door, listening to the rhythm of his speech, but could not make out the words. She thought he was most likely still asleep, and had returned to her bed – their bed – where she'd lain awake until dawn.

Crossing a ploughed field, helping him avoid the mud, she said, 'Which Mahler was it?'

'Five. The Death March.'

She laughed again; she couldn't help it.

'You see?' he said. 'You wouldn't believe it either.'

Was he sure, they'd said, that this young man – this twenty-year-old plasterer from Poland, in his work clothes, innocent and with no idea what was about to happen – was it likely that he'd have been listening to Mahler's Fifth Symphony? Was it likely that the shots the five policemen fired into the back of his head would match the rhythm of the music?

It was possible.

It was possible, certainly. But was it likely? Was it *credible?*

He didn't know, he could be wrong, but that was what he remembered.

They said if he could not be sure, it was best not to mention it.

They said the man was large, his clothes were not clean. He would have sat with his legs splayed, his large work boots planted firmly out in front of the adjoining seats: surely he would have noticed that?

It was almost raining again now. The damp air was soft, the light opaque, directionless. The fields looked larger than usual, flatter, deprived of any shadows. Sheep grazed listlessly. She pointed out, as she often had before, the regular corrugations, the thousand year-old marks left in the landscape by the strip farming of medieval peasants. They turned into the access road that led into the estate, and she felt the slight incline in the muscles of her legs. There were no real hills in this part of the country, but the road – and the new estate – cut hard across the contours of the land it occupied.

'Are you all right?' she said, when they were back indoors, their coats and boots left drying in the porch. 'That wasn't too much for you?'

'I'm fine. But I think I'll stay here this afternoon.'

The telephone rang while Stella was out. He considered letting it ring, but thought he'd better get used to this sometime. He found the phone and picked it up. It was light and cordless, like a mobile. He pressed the green button.

'Guy West.' He almost swallowed the unfamiliar name.

'Dad?'

It was Jason. His mind churned; he said nothing. Into the silence, Jason said, 'Hi. You're back.'

'Yes.'

'How are you feeling now?'

'I'm better than I was.'

There was a pause.

'That's good. Is Mum there?'

'No. No, she's in town, I'm afraid. Shopping.'

'Well, I hope she's getting plenty of food in. Turns out I can come tomorrow after all. Tell her I'll stay over, will you? There's nothing here I can't miss on Monday.'

'All right.'

'And tell her I'm sorry I couldn't make it for Bella's birthday, yeah? But I'll see her tomorrow, yeah?'

'Yes.'

'And you, Dad. Good to have you back.'

Stella said, 'You'll have to sleep with me tomorrow.'

'Why?'

'Because we've only got two bedrooms here. Because otherwise Jason will think there's something wrong. You know what the young are like.'

Over dinner that night, he told her everything. He didn't go to Wellingborough; he was not a redundant production manager. He was a witness. His name was Henry Fielding, and he had seen a man killed – executed – by five armed policemen on a Midland Mainline train. The man was unarmed. He was innocent – there had been some terrible mistake – but that was not the policemen's story.

She said, 'It's all right, Guy. I know.'

'I'm not Guy, I'm Henry. I'm a witness. I saw it.'

But what had he seen? In his sleep now, he told her, he sees the man's splayed thighs. His jeans are dirty. The right thigh, the one nearest to him, moves up and down to the rhythm of some unknown, unheard music; there is no Mahler, and his foot taps soundlessly, despite the heavy boot. Already, he said, he knows that what he sees is not what he saw.

In the night she heard his voice again.

She stood at the door, listening. She was wearing a long T-shirt; her legs and feet grew cold. She opened the door. It was dark, darker than her room, but she could make out his body, curled away from her. The duvet had slid, or been kicked, onto the floor. She picked it up, lay quickly on the bed and pulled it over both of them.

He did not move; his mumbling continued.

She rolled onto her side, pressed herself against him, fitting her knees into his, her breasts against his back, her left arm around his chest. She wondered where to put her other arm: lying this way there was never anywhere for it to go.

Gradually his murmuring subsided, then stopped. She managed to get comfortable, and they slept.

In the morning she woke before he did. He had rolled onto his front, his face pressed sideways into the pillow, one arm raised, the other trailing out behind him. He looked like the chalk outline of a murder victim from a film or the cover of a crime novel.

She smiled. Even asleep he was pretending, dramatising.

She rolled him onto his back. He felt surprisingly light. She examined his body as if she had never seen it before. She traced her finger along his sternum, felt ribs where before there had been soft, doughy flesh. The stomach was flatter, the hip bones more pronounced. The familiar bifurcated form of a man looked strange and new. As she continued her inspection, his penis stirred, grew, twitched and stood upright. She checked that he was still asleep, then stroked it gently, rubbing it with the smooth skin on the inside of her wrist. She knelt, leaned over and licked it tentatively, took it into her mouth, something she had not done for years. As he woke, she threw her leg across his thighs and sat up. She leaned forward until her face was close to his, his penis pressed against her belly.

'Henry,' she whispered. 'Wake up.'

She kissed him on the mouth.

'How would you like your eggs, Henry?'

When Jason arrived, Henry – watching from the kitchen where they'd left the door ajar – thought at first that he looked a little like the Polish plasterer. This happened a lot.

Jason was fair, not dark, his hair long and almost curly, his chin half-covered by a ragged beard, where the Pole had been clean-shaven; but they had the same loose-limbed physical confidence. The same way of more than filling the space they occupied. Watching him, Henry thought it obvious that he could not have spawned this blond monster. Jason was nearly a foot taller than his mother, but she was strong and when they embraced in the hallway they did so vigorously, as equals. When they released each other, Jason turned towards the kitchen, towards Henry, arms outstretched.

Instinctively, he stepped backwards, but Jason was only shrugging the small backpack from his shoulders.

Stella said, 'Jason, I'm sorry. Didn't you get my message?'

'Sorry, Mum, my mobile's died. What was it? Did you want me to pick something up on the way here?'

She said, 'You can't stay. In fact, you can't come in.'

She told him she was sorry, that his dad had thought he'd be OK but, now it came to it, he wasn't. He wasn't up to seeing anyone yet, not even Jason.

'But Mum…'

She told him not to worry, she'd be all right. She told him to stay locally, in town – she gave him some cash. She'd meet him tomorrow, at work.

She pushed him out, still protesting. She locked the door and turned, leaning against it, as Henry emerged from the kitchen. She laughed, wild and raw, a sound that shocked them both for a moment. Then they collided, Stella tearing at his clothes, struggling to shrug off her jeans, Henry holding her face in both hands, kissing her mouth desperately.

'Henry,' she said, later. 'When's the trial?'

He was half-asleep. The sun, low in the early afternoon, sliced through the blinds, lighting corrugated strips on the duvet. Her head was on his shoulder, her hair spread across his chest.

He said, 'Trial?'

'You know, the trial.'

'Oh. Sometime in the spring, maybe. They weren't sure.'

She pressed herself closer, her leg hooked across his waist, her groin sticky against his thigh.

'And you'll still need protection, won't you? When it's over?'

'They didn't say.'

'But they couldn't just abandon you?'

He said nothing for a while. 'I suppose not.'

Stella smiled and rubbed her cheek against his chest. She said, 'Henry, you're married, aren't you?'

He looked at her. 'Oh yes.'

'Then I suppose this can't last.'

He didn't reply.

'Do you have children?'

'Yes,' he said, not realising the stakes. 'A boy and a girl.'

Her body had stiffened against his; neither of them said anything more.

In the morning, before she left for work, he told her about the Mahler again. He *had* heard Mahler. It might not be credible, but it was true. Hurrying to get out of the house, she said, 'I know, Guy. You've told me before.'

In the house on the edge of the estate, he wondered who this Guy West was, anyway? When they'd cast around for an identity to hide him in, how had they alighted upon this public schoolboy failure – with the dead daughter and the giant of a son and the sexy, tiring wife? He couldn't have been completely clean. He must have been *known*; they had to have been aware that he was ill, that he might die, that Stella would co-operate. He assumed the answer lay somewhere in India, or – more likely – Pakistan. It was not the most stable part of the world these days.

But it didn't really matter who Guy was, he thought. I might as well be him: at least until it's time to take the stand.

# Weathering

WHEN HE SAYS, 'You're beautiful,' he does so not because it is true – which, even allowing for the fact that beauty is to some extent in the eye of the beholder, it is not – nor because he nonetheless believes it to be true – which, with all the opportunities for comparison their metropolitan life together in a media-saturated age affords, he does not – and not because he thinks she will believe it – for she lives, after all, in the same environment as he, and has the same opportunities for comparative analysis – nor even that she will believe that he believes it – surely she must, by this time, know him better than that? – but, in the end, because he wants it to be true. He wants, despite the evidence of his senses and the cold hard facts, not to feel that he has pledged himself to a life of mediocrity, a life in which he will never sail single-handedly around the world, will never drink himself to death, will never paint a picture, never write a poem, a song, a string quartet so breath-taking that it freezes time and brings tyrants, weeping, to their knees, will never know, will never hold, will never love, a beautiful woman; he does not want that to be his story. So he gets up close, he nuzzles his face into her neck, he gets so close he cannot really see her, and what he sees he cannot focus on, and he says: 'You're beautiful.'

When she says, 'No I'm not,' she does so not because what he says is not true – although, even allowing for the fact that beauty is at least in part in the eye of the beholder, it is not – nor because she does not believe it to be true – although, for the reasons explained above, she does not – nor even because she believes that he believes it to be true and is in need of some correction – for she knows him better than that – but, when all is said and done, because she thinks of it as a gift, a flower, a diamond, or a pair of socks, as something that has its own meaning, beyond the words themselves. She likes to hear him say it, she wants him to say it again and she believes – with some justice – that if she says, 'I know,' or even simply fails to contradict him, she will – given the available evidence and opportunities for comparative analysis – appear vain, or even slightly mad, and, even though he may not want to, he will notice this and think her vain, or slightly mad, and will not be able to say it again, even though he wants to, and a rift would open up between them. The rift would be small, at first, a crack no wider than a finger, no wider than a hair, but when the rains came it would fill with water, and when the cold came it would freeze, then thaw, then freeze and the rock would split apart. Over time a vast boulder would be reduced to a small stone surrounded by rubble. At school they called it weathering, teaching her the way mountains rise and crumble, the way the hardest, most solid objects fall apart. Her friends said geography was for losers, but she knew what to guard against.

So when he says, 'You're beautiful' it is true, and they believe it; and when she says, 'No I'm not,' that is true, too.

# In Plain Sight

I DIDN'T KNOW there was anyone watching, didn't know you could even hide a spy round here, on the back of the mountain, where there aren't even any trees. But Jeannie said that wasn't how it worked. Spies don't really hide, she said. They're the ones you see but don't see. All I could see was chickens, and the goats up at Jeannie's farm; and Jeannie, of course. And then once in a blue moon – election time – a politician's armoured car might shoulder its way up here, carrying soldiers.

But there were spies, and someone told them about me. And they, the spies, told their counterparts in another country on the other side of the world, who told their general, and the general told the President, who told the people all the way over there on the other side of the world that I was evil.

I didn't know that's what they were saying for a week or so because I didn't have satellite. I had chickens. Jeannie had satellite and a generator she ran a couple of hours a day. On a Friday I'd collect my eggs and climb up to Jeannie's farm where the ground was steep and hard and nothing grew but lichen and goats. How the goats found enough to fill their udders I never knew, but Jeannie milked them and made crumbly, pungent cheese that kept some texture when it melted and made a first-class omelette. Jeannie would pass the eggs we didn't eat to a man on the other side of the mountain who had a car (a 1970's Mercedes saloon he'd won in a bet, she said, from a taxi driver down on the alluvial plain) and who swapped the eggs for spinach and pepper and medicine.

Every Friday I'd put on my shirt, lick my fingers to straighten my hair, scrape a knife under my nails and haul a basket up to Jeannie's. She'd crack a few eggs into a bowl and

15

beat them, then wilt the spinach she got from the man with the Mercedes. There was more water there, she said, and better soil; he'd even grown watercress once, before the soldiers diverted the river. But spinach, with perhaps a bit of pepper when she had it, was almost as good. She'd crumble cheese and fry the eggs, scraping the pan a little with a fork. I'd talk about my chickens: which were laying, which were heading for the pot. She'd put the omelette on the table and we'd sit either side, a fork each, picking it straight out of the hot pan. She'd say it wasn't her best and I'd contradict her; she'd dip cups into a pitcher of milk to wash it down.

Then one night the cup came up full of wine. I hadn't drunk wine since the last time the soldiers came. Jeannie had danced on the table and kissed the would-be Mayor; I had picked a fight with a bodyguard and probably would have died if Jeannie hadn't pulled him off. Now the wine went to my head and made me talk too loudly, and when we went to bed I couldn't. Jeannie said it didn't matter and we fell asleep with her long hard arms around my chest.

In the morning Jeannie asked if it was true that I was evil. I asked her what she meant, what they were saying about us.

'Not us, buster. You. You're a threat.'

She told me the President of a far-off country had gone on television and told her people that my way of life was incompatible with theirs. I was a threat to their security.

'How am I a threat?'

'You tell me.'

I reached for her. The early morning sunlight slanted through the empty window, picking out the tiny hairs on her work-hard limbs. She slapped my hand away lightly. 'I've got goats to milk,' she said. 'Besides, you're evil.'

At home that afternoon I tried not to let my worry show. Chickens aren't bright, but they are sensitive. They contract anxiety and share it among themselves like a mutant virus. I soothed them with music from a tiny FM radio the man with the Mercedes and the watercress had given to

Jeannie, and Jeannie had given to me, in return for half a picture she said she wanted, the only one I had.

Chickens like Bach best of all, hate modern jazz and news, so I had to pay attention and keep re-tuning. I found a B-minor Mass that night, which should have been perfect, but perhaps I played it too loud, or I missed an interval discussion on Ornette Coleman, because in the morning when I scattered the feed and picked through the litter, there were less than half the eggs there should have been. The following day there were fewer still. It wasn't the music, I knew: it was me. I had to do something, but what? I lived on the back of a mountain surrounded by other mountains. I lived on eggs and the things I could swap eggs for.

That Friday I cleaned my nails, stuck down my hair, and climbed the mountainside to Jeannie's with the few eggs I could muster. After dinner, I showed Jeannie a letter I had written.

> '*Dear Madam President,*' she read aloud in a voice that wasn't her voice, or my voice, '*We haven't met, but I know that you have heard of me, and you know that I keep chickens. Would you like some eggs? I have nothing else.*'

I didn't know the President's address, but I figured that, if I could get the letter to her country, it would find its way to her.

Jeannie said it wouldn't work; she said I did not understand these people. All the same, I asked her to carry the letter to the man with a Mercedes, and ask him to drive it down to where there might be a Post Office and he could post it for me. Jeannie said the man's car had a broken drive shaft. It had been broken for almost a year: since the watercress business died he could no longer afford the spares. Besides, she said, the roads were now so bad he'd need a four-wheel drive, a jeep maybe, to get spares up here; and even then, he wouldn't be able to drive the Mercedes anywhere but round his farmyard. I asked what had been happening to my eggs. She said the man knew another man, a bit further down the mountain, who had a mule. For a box of eggs the man without a car would take the letter to the man with the mule, who, for more eggs, might take it down to the plain and find a Post Office.

So I gave her the letter, and the few eggs I had; there were none left for our omelette, so we had a little cheese and some spinach salad. When we went to bed that night Jeannie said she was tired and would I just hold her? We lay together with my belly pressed tight and warm against her long back, my knees tucked behind her knees, my face pressed into her hair, my prick curled and small like a grub. She said, 'What are you going to do?'

To the back of her head, to her hair, I said, 'The President will like my eggs.'

'She won't want your eggs.'

'No?'

'You're an affront to the values of her people. That's what she said. You're making no attempt to adapt your way of life. She said they could not tolerate that.'

'She said that?'

Jeannie didn't answer.

'What does it mean?'

Jeannie rolled away from me. 'They're sending an aircraft carrier.'

'I live on a mountain.'

'They have missiles. Their General said they have missiles so smart they can ring your doorbell before they march right in and blow you to dust.'

'I don't have a doorbell.'

Jeannie pinched out the candle and pretended to sleep.

In the morning I reached for her, but the bed was empty. I got up quickly. On the table was a postcard propped against a cup of goat's milk. The card read:

> *Dear Stan,*
> *I am taking your letter and your eggs to the man on the other*

*side of the mountain who may pass it on. If there is a reply,*
*I will bring it to you. In the meantime, I don't think you*
*should come here again.*
*I'm sorry.*
*Love, Jeannie.*
*PS Help yourself to milk (and wine).*

I turned the card over. On the front was a picture of a lush green field. White lettering read: *Weedon's Watercress. Since 1854.*

I drank the milk. I was about to leave when I noticed the television in the corner of the room. It was television that had told Jeannie I was evil. She had showed me how it worked a long time ago, but always said there was nothing worth watching on a Friday night. Now I fired up the generator and turned the TV on. I flipped through the channels: hospitals and cops, a singer, cops, hospitals, cops. Finally I found a woman in a cardigan talking across a vast glass desk to a man in glasses and a button-down shirt. On a wall-sized screen behind her, another man stood outside a large public building, his hair and the flags behind him snapping in a stiff breeze. A message scrolled across the bottom of the screen: *Why does Stan hate us?*

The woman swivelled her chair to talk to the man on the studio screen. 'Erwin Moss, is that how you see it?'

There was a slight pause while he fiddled in his ear. 'I'm sorry, Kirsty, I couldn't…'

'Do you agree that envy is at the heart of this issue?' She stressed the words *agree, envy, heart.*

Another, slighter pause, then the man on the screen said, 'I think it is, Kirsty. Stan looks down from that mountain and sees everything we've got. He sees universal internet access, advanced medical systems, cherry frappuccino. He sees the incredible freedoms we enjoy, and he is simply consumed by envy.'

'Really? Does he even *care* about us?'

'Hell yes, he cares. What's he got? Chicken. Eggs, maybe. Dirt. Of course he cares. He hates us.'

The woman swung back to the man in the studio. 'Mark Speen, I believe you've actually spent *time* with Stan?'

The man took his glasses off, polished them on his shirt as he spoke. 'Not with Stan himself, Kirsty. But on Stan's mountain, with Jeannie. And I have to say that she's actually a lovely, lovely person. She keeps goats, makes terrific cheese.'

'What did she *tell* you about *Stan*?'

'She said he keeps himself pretty much to himself. Brings her eggs sometimes. But basically he's a very private person.'

The woman swung back towards the screen. 'Isn't that the *problem*, Erwin?'

A slight pause, a finger in the ear. 'That's the problem, Kirsty, in a nutshell. Stan's a loner. Doesn't want to join the twenty-first century. Plays a *lot* of classical music. And God knows what he's cooking up in that hut of his.'

The man in the studio said, 'Erwin is just scare-mongering. Ask him what happens next.'

'What *does* happen, next?'

The man on the screen said, 'We let it go, Kirsty, he's won.'

The woman looked straight at the camera, straight at me, and said: 'Is it *envy*? Or something else? Tell us why *you* think Stan hates us.' As she spoke, the studio dissolved behind a torn black-and-white photograph. It took me a moment to recognise my wedding picture. I had the other half at home, the half with my wife in it. On the television was the half I'd given Jeannie.

I took the wine and went home.

The following Friday I put on my shirt, stayed at home and drank the wine. It was a cloudy, moonless night, too dark to see. When the wine was all gone, I was sick.

I awoke to the sound of rain and an unfamiliar grinding noise. I raised my head from the floor, and put my hand in the sick. It was cold and thin. I heard light footsteps, a heavy click, an engine. Through a hole in the kitchen wall I saw a white-haired man pulling away in a Range Rover. Lying in the doorway I found a letter. It said:

> *Stan,*
> *Don't think you can get round our democracy with eggs. The President has her own eggs. You have twenty-four hours to love us.*
> *General Weedon.*

I fed the chickens, found a St Matthew Passion on the radio and headed up the mountain. Climbing, I watched the Range Rover round up dust clouds; it dragged them through the pass and out of sight.

Jeannie's door was shut. I hammered on it. I banged on the window, and broke it. I'd never understood the fragility of glass before, its lacerating edge. From inside, Jeannie said, 'I told you not to come here.'

I held out the letter, my arm through the window, percolating blood into her sink. 'Read it, please.'

She shook her head, but she took the letter, read it. 'The bastard,' she said.

'They're going to kill me.'

Jeannie bit her lip, shut her eyes. Then she said, 'Come in, quickly.'

She bandaged my arm, gave me milk and bread to settle my stomach, a pill for the pain in my head. I asked her what it was, what it would do; she told me just to take it, that it would work. She'd got it from Weedon. Then she told me about Weedon, how he'd saved his farm after the river was diverted, how he was driving a Range Rover now, the promises he'd made. I told her about my wife, then, about the way I'd watched her skin become hard, translucent, like a shell.

I said, 'What am I going to do?'

'Stay with me.'

'What about the chickens?'

'We can fetch them in the morning. We'll keep them here.'

In the night I heard noises I told myself were goats. I held Jeannie until I fell asleep.

In the morning we woke to find Jeannie's farm surrounded by a concrete wall. It was grey and twice as high as me; along the top the blades of razor wire caught the sun, made stars against the lightening sky. There were no gates, no doors, no windows.

Jeannie milked the goats, fired up the generator. On TV a man with a lapel badge stood outside a building with a lot of flags. He said: 'Frankly, we're done talking. Evidently, Stan doesn't want a solution. He wants to stick his albumin-based lifestyle down all our throats.'

A voice off camera said, 'But is a blockade going to *help*? Won't it just *punish* the innocent? Like Jeannie and the goats?'

'Well, now, Jeannie, I've got to say, Jeannie has made her bed and she'll have to lie in it, with whomever. That's her choice. In a free world, like ours, Kirsty, that's her choice and we have to respect that. As for the goats, young lady – hell, I know goats. Goats are tough. It'll take more than a Peace Wall to finish them off.'

Nothing much happened for a while. We milked the goats, ate cheese. The wall followed the perimeter of Jeannie's land scrupulously, crossing and re-crossing a stream in the south east corner. We drank fresh water and, in the evenings when the sun had lost its rage and the rocks gently pulsed back the day's heat, we bathed together. At night, when we could no longer see, we made love.

One day, while we were bathing, we heard the sound of trucks beyond the north wall, then the clanking of metal poles. We dressed hurriedly, retreated to the house. Presently we saw men in green uniforms and yellow hats hauling huge black boxes onto the top of the wall. Then the music started.

Jeannie said she'd always liked 'Imagine'. She sang along with her eyes closed, imagining no countries, imagining all the people living lives in peace. Then the song ended. And started again. Before it had finished for the second time, a second stack of loudspeakers appeared on the opposite wall. As John Lennon, from the north, began imagining for a third time, we held our breath, waiting to see what would come from the south. It was 'Lucy in the Sky with Diamonds'. By William Shatner. Jeannie stopped singing.

From then on only the volume changed. For most of the time the music played comfortably, if repetitively, at a level one might choose oneself. Then, without warning, both songs would drop, mid-chorus, to a whisper we had to strain to hear, even though we didn't want to hear them, even though we thought we'd slit each other's throats if we heard them one more time. Then we'd be forced to wait for the sound to vault to a level that made plates shiver across the table and loosened the eyeballs in our heads.

The effect on the goats was devastating. At first, we observed, they learned to cope with the discord and the repetition by huddling together right under the north stack, where Lennon all but drowned out Shatner; then, as the piano chords faded, they would gallop across to the south stack to hear 'Lucy in the Sky with Diamonds' almost uncontaminated by 'Imagine'. The tactic left little time or space to graze, however; weakened by hunger, most were soon standing rooted to the spot, heads bowed, beards brushing the rocks as they swayed endlessly from side to side.

The milk dried up by morning. We ran out of cheese the following day.

'Imagine there's no hunger,' said Jeannie, and I could have strangled her there and then.

I said, 'What are we going to eat?'

Jeannie looked around. Then she said: 'Goat.'

She said we should start with a billy. She picked one out, rocking his head to Shatner. She looped a rope around his legs and pulled it tight, put the bucket on a flat rock. I caught him by the horns, and we forced him down. Under a marmalade sky Jeannie slit his throat, while I strained to keep the dying goat from tearing free, his hooves from lashing out and overturning the bucket. When she'd had all the blood she was going to get, Jeannie rolled him on his back and slit his belly, tugging her knife up towards his ribs. A girl with kaleidoscope eyes. She pulled a slick of purple viscera out onto the warm rock. The first flies arrived moments later.

I said, 'We can't leave that here. Should we bury it?'

Jeannie stamped her foot. Her studded boots flashed sparks off the rock.

'We could wash it down the stream,' I said.

Jeannie shook her head. 'We'd poison the water supply for miles.'

In the end we wrapped the entrails in an old sheet, butchered the meat and waited for dark. Singing our own words to 'Lucy in the Sky with Diamonds' we carried the bundle, alive with flies and dripping viscous fluid, to the west wall. We threw it over. Then we ate goat curry and made love.

Just before dawn the music was quiet and I was woken by a soft, liquid thud outside, then another, and another and a louder thud as something hit the roof. It sounded as if it were raining wet towels. As the first light crept over the east wall I could see the bare rock of Jeannie's farm transformed into an undulating mulch of decomposing chicken carcasses. Outside, in the yard, I tried to pick one up; it was so rotten it tore apart under its own weight, scattering maggots at my feet. More chickens were being flung – catapulted? – over the walls, describing perfect parabolas before squelching into the rocks, the house. Jeannie came out to find me and caught one full in the chest; it disintegrated, spattering her with putrefying filth. She staggered under the blow, then turned back indoors, tearing the clothes from her body.

She fired up the generator – we were almost out of fuel, now – and pressed the TV control buttons frantically. The stations skipped and fizzed until Jeannie fixed upon a woman in a jacket with hard edges and stitching you could see, who was saying – in a voice we could just hear above those of

Lennon and Shatner – that Governor Weedon had claimed there had been a unilateral escalation of the crisis; that, during the night, troops guarding the Peace Wall had come under biological attack. The Governor was reported as saying, 'We've given Stan every opportunity, but this is not the sort of thing we tolerate in a free world.' The woman in the jacket said global financial markets had reacted positively to the Governor's promise of imminent, resolute action.

I looked at Jeannie. She was hunched over the TV control, rocking back and forth, her eyes glazed, like a goat. The generator spluttered and quit, the picture faded. Jeannie rocked, her teeth locked, shivering; sweat spangled her forehead. I held her, felt the heat of her fever. I put her to bed under a thin sheet, hunted for the pills she'd given me. I found them in the basket where she'd kept spinach. They were multivitamins. I gave her a couple anyway. The rain of chickens eased, then stopped.

By midday the temperature outside was a hundred and ten. The stench was thick, like paint. I had to tie a cloth around my face to keep from breathing flies. I laid the sheet over Jeannie's head, but it looked like a shroud and I pulled it off, fanned the flies away instead. She had stopped rocking and begun talking. She talked about her husband, about possessions, about Weedon, about her family, about cellophane flowers, about the sea, the wind, the grass, about me. About heaven and hell. None of it made any sense. Before the sun went down again she was dead.

It is cloudy outside now; it should be dark, but I can see, because the soldiers have set lamps around the walls and the mountain is filled with flat, white light. I go back indoors, upend a cupboard, tipping its meagre contents all over the floor, shattering cups and plates. I stamp on the cupboard, smashing it to pieces. I do the same to the table. Then I take the rope we'd used to tether the goat and, as best I can, I lash together a ladder. Outside again, I grub amongst the carcasses, brush flies from half a dozen that, while rotten enough, can yet be held up by the feet without falling apart; I tie them to the rope and string them, like bandoliers, across my chest. I throw a blanket over my shoulders and carry my makeshift ladder over to the west wall.

As I reach the top, a spotlight swings to pick me out. Blinded, I hear rather than see the soldiers readying their weapons.

'Hold your fire!'

Shielding my eyes against the glare, I see a white-haired man in a spotless uniform stepping through the ranks. Epaulettes and braid adorn his body like Christmas decorations.

'Stan?' he says. 'I'm Governor Weedon.' He makes a gesture and the music abruptly ceases, leaving silence roaring in my ears. He waits. I look down at the soldiers, each with a rifle pointed at my chest or my head. I throw off the blanket, hear the soldiers' breath stop.

I say, 'What do you want from me?'

'We want you to love us, Stan.'

I say, 'I love you.'

'Really?'

I take a deep breath, thinking of the chickens, thinking of Jeannie's goats, of Jeannie gabbling about heaven and hell. I say, 'Really.'

Weedon orders his men to lower their weapons, steps towards the wall. 'Well, heck, Stan,' he says, 'why didn't you say so earlier?'

He is standing right below me now, head tipped back, looking up. Before he can move I drop a chicken right onto his face. I watch it split apart and fill his mouth. He retches and spits rancid flesh and maggots and a long trail of saliva onto the rock at his feet. He looks up and I can see the fear in his eyes, the anger and the hatred; it warms me. I hold up two more carcasses as the rifles rise and fire and the bullets come my way. I watch them come, spinning in the artificial light, racing to destroy me. I see the first one strike, feel it tugging at my clothes and flesh. I feel the second, and the third, and I know that it is bliss to be alive.

# Do I Know You?

1

HE WALKED UP from the market, passing the clothes shops and the buskers, picking his way through groups of teens mustering outside the tube. One woman, older than most of the tourists around her, stood alone on the corner. Without intending to, he thought: so-so. Legs a bit short.

As he edged past, she said: Excuse me, are you Joe?

She was holding a rolled up *Time Out*. Her mouth was nice – small, but OK. It didn't bleed into the rest of her face like some. Her denim jacket was tight where it was buttoned over her breasts. Her hair was dark and long, pulled back from her face. He liked that.

– Joe? she said again. Are you Joe?

He heard himself say: I could be.

She turned away, towards the tube station. He found he wanted her to turn back again.

– This Joe, what do you know about him?

She turned. She looked him up and down, not hiding it. She said: OK. Let's get a drink.

They went to the pub just across from the station. It was large, with mismatched chairs and saggy leather sofas. Each table had a small brass number plate recessed into the surface.

Joe ordered white wine and a pint of Fosters.

He watched the barmaid. She was tiny. Perfect. Black jeans, a tight black tee, a little white apron tied around her hips.

The woman who wanted him to be Joe was watching him. He said: What's your name, anyway?

She paused before she said, Elizabeth.

– There you go, Liz. He handed her the wineglass.

They walked over to a table. He drank, swallowing twice without taking the glass from his mouth. She sipped her wine quietly. She seemed to be waiting for something. He drained his glass and stood to buy a second pint; she insisted it was her round, even though she hadn't finished her wine. He wondered what to talk about when she came back. He'd never been picked up by a woman before.

He watched her at the bar, saying something to the man next to her. She wasn't bad. She laughed, shook her head and pointed back at Joe. The man saw Joe watching them, faked a grin and waved, just from the wrist, then turned away.

He watched her walk back towards him, threading through the tables. She rose up on her toes and sucked her stomach in to squeeze past some fat bloke who wouldn't move his chair. Nice, thought Joe. Not up there with the barmaid, but nice all the same. He'd underestimated her. She'd look good in heels.

She put the second pint in front of him, sat down.

– Who was the guy at the bar?

– No one.

– It wasn't Joe?

She smiled. Aren't you Joe?

He swallowed a mouthful of lager. She took her time.

– It was just a guy in a bar.

She finished her wine, placed the empty glass in front of him.

– Are we going to eat, then, she said, or what?

2

Later, at her flat, Joe asked about the fish. They were everywhere: some alive, in a couple of tanks, dodging in and out of plastic caves; some dead, stuffed, in Victorian glass and mahogany cases; there were sculptures of fish; fish-based designs on posters and cushion covers; even, Joe had discovered, shiny metallic fish set in the transparent Perspex toilet seat.

– My flatmate's keen on fish.

– No kidding, said Joe. He thought: Flatmate?

She must have caught the look on his face.

– Helen. She's not here.

– Right.

– I mean, she's not *here*. She's in... Switzerland.

– Switzerland?

– Skiing.

– In July?

– Or walking. Probably walking.

She took her jacket off, threw it on a chair; she pulled the long sleeves of her top down over the backs of her hands, gripped them against her palms. She fussed with a packet of cigarettes, offered him a drink.

He said, I think I've had enough.

He'd had more than enough. He was only here because he was a man, and women didn't pick him up and take him home, but this one had, and now he was drunk and not at all sure he knew what he was doing here.

– Right, she said. Tea?

While she was gone, he scanned the CDs. He couldn't see anything he'd buy himself. Among the books he saw some Hardy, some Eliot. Virginia Woolf. Stuff he hadn't read since college. There was poetry, too: Wordsworth, Duffy, Donne. Robert Lowell. A biography of Lorca. A Bible. A Spanish dictionary. He heard a teapot lid click into place and sat down hastily.

Coming back into the living room she stood in the doorway for a moment, watching him. She said, What did you see?

He shrugged. Books.

She poured two mugs of tea, sat down beside him on the sofa.

– What do they tell you?

– You like poetry?

She laughed. Is that it?

The way she said it, it didn't sound like small talk. But

he had no idea what she wanted. He said, You did English at university? You speak Spanish? Yeah?

– Yeah. So what does that say about me?

Joe shook his head, sipped his tea.

– Make me up, Joe.

– What?

– I could be anybody you like. Make me up. Like a story.

– I'm no good at stories.

– Yes you are. Now make something up for me.

He wasn't sure he liked the way this was going. He looked Lizzie over again. The hair; the mouth; the breasts; her knees pulled up and pressed against them. Would she be worth it? What would she want?

He lit a cigarette, offered her one. She shook her head.

– OK. OK, you're… Elizabeth. You're… twenty-eight?

– Thirty-two, actually, but thank you.

– Thirty-two. You're single, but you'd rather not be. You live with a girlfriend.

– You know this. I want you to make something up.

– OK…

She crossed her arms around her knees. There were holes in her sleeves; she'd hooked her thumbs through the holes, pulling the wool tight over her wrists and palms. He'd known girls who did that before. A girl. Joe closed his eyes. He'd been in a car once, with a mate driving, and he could see they were going to crash and he couldn't do a thing but watch. It felt like that, now. He said, You tried to kill yourself, once.

He heard her shifting on the sofa, and opened his eyes.

– I did? Why?

After a moment, he said: A boy, of course.

– I wasn't very original, then?

– No, but you meant it. You still have the scars on your wrists. And they're vertical, the way the veins flow. The way you do it when you mean it.

She let that hang in the air a moment.

– Who was the boy?

30

– He was called Jo... nah. Jonah. Your first real boyfriend. At school, sixth form. He was in the year above you. He was... what was he?

– You tell me.

He'd be whatever I'm not, Joe thought.

– He was... a poet. Yeah, a poet. He ran the school magazine. He was tall and thin – a pretty boy, with huge brown eyes. He wore those little string bracelets on his wrists, second-hand waistcoats. In your school, he was very, very cool. You thought he looked like... Shelley.

She laughed.

He carried on: There was a big old mole on his left buttock nobody in school knew about but you – you and a dozen other girls, that is.

She tutted, so he said: Plus the headmaster's secretary and the guy who taught medieval history. He – Jonah – took you to a party. You were over the moon. You drank a bottle of wine. It was warm and you went out into the garden. He rolled a joint, and you knew you were in love. He...

Joe inhaled deeply on his cigarette; he coughed and smoke came out of his mouth and nose at the same time. How was he going to say this?

– He... took your virginity.

Not missing a beat, she said, Did it hurt?

Hurt? Joe asked himself again: what did she want? He said, I don't know. Does it?

– It's your story, Joe.

– OK. It hurt. But you didn't care. In fact, you liked it. You liked the fact it hurt. It made you feel... Victorian. Overwhelmed by forbidden passion, like a Brontë. Like it mattered. But then he dumped you. You wrote a poem about it; loads of poems. But the bastard wouldn't print them in the school magazine and you hated him. But you couldn't hate him, could you? You were seventeen. So you loved him, and hated yourself instead.

He stubbed out his cigarette, mashing it into the ashtray.

She clapped, and said, Very good.

– Was I close?

– That's not the point. You entertained me.

– Is that the point?

He felt drained. He needed to get his breath back, but she asked for more.

More? She'd really better be worth it. He closed his eyes and tried to picture her ten, fifteen years younger.

– After Jonah, after you got out of hospital, you went away for a bit, stayed with an aunt in Bognor.

– How exotic.

– You spent the summer there. When you got back to school, you wore long sleeves. It was September and Jonah had gone off to university – no, he'd pissed off to the Far East on a gap year. Finding himself. You didn't want anything to do with boys in any case. Or poetry. Whenever your teachers got onto shepherds and nymphs you yawned so loud the whole class could hear. You kept that up until...

He had talked himself into a corner. Until what? He had no idea what he was going to say next.

– Until what?

He watched one of the fish sucking filth from the side of the tank.

– Until you got to go to Venice on a foreign language exchange with Benedetta, and you slept with her father, while she was out playing around with boys your own age.

Joe was back on a roll, enjoying himself now.

– After that, you went to uni, and let a string of vegetarian shoe-gazers into your bed. They were all so up themselves they didn't last long, but one or two were really needy and totally deaf when you wanted to ditch them. So you took up with Charlie. Charlie was forty, an ex-butcher turned animal rights campaigner. You thought you could help him with his issues. But, just after you met him, he broke into the university labs to liberate some beagles, left his bus pass behind, and got three years. You went to visit him whenever you could. You hated the prison, but loved... He paused.

What would she have loved? He said, You thought he was a peasant: simple; honest. You loved that. All the same, you were glad he couldn't touch you any more with those big, butcher's hands. After a year or so, though, duty called: you thought you ought to ask about conjugal visits. The warders laughed themselves stupid and said that was for his wife, and she'd be none too pleased.

– Goodness. You don't think much of me, do you?

– It's your game, Lizzie. Hang in there, though, it might get better.

– You never know, she said.

Where was he? Outside the prison gates, with the sound of laughter ringing in Lizzie's ears. What more did she want? He said: After Charlie you thought about killing yourself again. All the time. He'd left you a delivery bike. With the diddy front wheel and the basket? You used to wobble about the streets on it, wondering how quickly oncoming trucks could stop. But then you got a job.

– What was I good at?

Joe looked up at a shelf above the door to the kitchen, and stared a trout in the eye. The trout must have been stuffed about a century before he was even born.

– You worked for a charity, the Mines Advisory Group. You were working with people who risked their lives in war zones all over the world. Not you, of course. Your JD said Executive Assistant – a glorified office gopher with no chance to use the Spanish and Italian that got you the job in the first place. But you didn't care. It was *real*, you thought: you could feel all nice and guilty and self-righteous. You liked that. Then Princess Di took up the cause and it got sexy for a while. And you enjoyed that, too, and hated yourself for enjoying it, because you thought you despised her.

– I like that. Carry on.

– Then Diana died and you met Peter – your rock, you said. Peter was one of MAG's in-country advisers. Ex-defence industry, till his conscience got to him; clever bastard with a fat passport and a perma-tan. You couldn't resist; you didn't want to resist. He said he loved your scars; in bed he used to lick them while you… made love. You gave him the best part of your twenties. Mind you, he was always away – Africa, Cambodia – more than he was with you. And every time he went, you'd go to church…

She shuddered. Was I a lefty or a Christian?

– Both. Neither. You hadn't been to church since you were a kid, but you went then. You went to church, and prayed – prayed he'd come back, that you'd see him again.

– For the last six months you didn't hear from him at all, but you prayed and prayed. You were convinced he was dead. No – you'd have heard. You were convinced he was maimed. Tortured. Rotting in a Khmer Rouge camp, having his extremities sliced off one by one, when, in fact, he was holed up in Bali with a nurse from New Zealand, dealing prescription morphine to Western tourists too scared to buy stuff off the locals. When that nightclub bomb went off, he was there. And there he was – bits of him, anyway – scattered right across the front pages. You couldn't miss the bastard. You stopped going to church. You stopped praying, because now you knew you had to be scared of getting what you pray for.

Joe stopped, wondering if he'd gone too far. Lizzie's head had dropped; her chin was sunk deep into the cushion she was cradling, her knees drawn up to meet it. He could hear the air bubbling through the fish tanks. Then she made a sound, an indeterminate murmur, and Joe thought she was going to cry. What had he said?

– Lizzie? he said. It's only a story.

The noise she was making became lighter, more rhythmic, and he realised she was laughing, after a fashion. She sprang up, flung her arms out and threw the cushion at his head. He turned to face her; she looked straight at him, held his eye.

– Good, Joe. Excellent.

He was relieved, pleased, stupidly pleased, then he caught himself feeling pleased and decided he was being patronised.

– God, but you like your women vulnerable, don't you?

Joe didn't say anything. He didn't know. It might even be true.

She stood directly in front of him, held her arms out, hands and elbows pressed together, wrists turned up for him to see. Running horizontally across each arm were five, six, seven scars, pale, faded to the colour of old limestone.

– Do you like them, Joe?

He felt as if his stomach was fighting to get out of his throat.

– I'm sorry, he managed to say.

– Don't be. You're not responsible. You like them, don't you?

What could he say?

He said, No! But that wasn't right. It sounded rude; and, besides, the truth was that he did.

– Feel them, Joe.

She pushed her arms closer. He took them carefully in both hands, ran his thumbs gently over the nub of the scars.

– Do you want to lick them?

He dropped her hands. He couldn't speak. Swiftly, before he could react, she straddled his knees, hands clasped around his neck. He could feel the smooth, corrugated flesh of her wrists pressed against his cheeks. Her breasts were level with his eyes.

Joe felt trapped, afraid, embarrassed, excited.

– What happens next?

– What?

– In the story. You can make it up.

Joe reached up, laid his hands on her shoulders, and looked up to her face, stopping at the mouth. He said:

– Joseph reached up. He laid his hands on Lizzie's shoulders...

– Give her another name. She paused. Like, Helen.

– Your flatmate? The one in Switzerland?

– It's just a name.

She inched herself a bit closer on his lap. Joe was aware of the warmth of her body where she sat, on his thighs. Aware his cock was hard. With one hand, he stroked her cheek; he put the other on her waist, judging, for the first time, the solidity, the heft of her body. She was real, she was here. He could touch her, feel the density of her flesh, the sharpness of her bones. He looked, at last, at her eyes, and saw them watching him.

He said, Jo…seph looked into her eyes, and he said, 'Sorry, Helen. I can't do this.'

– But Helen said, 'You can.'

– Joseph shook his head sadly. He said, 'Really. I'm sorry.'

She watched him for a moment. He knew she could feel the fear in his hands, the violence in his eyes. She climbed off his lap.

– OK, she said. Go on. Get out.

He stood up. He waited for her to say something else. She picked up the tea pot and the empty mugs and carried them into the kitchen. He heard the sound of water running in the sink. He left.

3

They met again, of course. After a week, she rang, asked him why he hadn't rung.

He said, You threw me out.

He couldn't ring. He had wondered what he'd do if she called him. Turn her down, he thought. But then she rang and named a restaurant. She told him to be there and he was.

– Let's go to your place, she said, after they'd eaten. He was surprised. He'd assumed that they'd go back to hers again.

When he showed her in, she said, Oh.

He asked her what that meant.

– Nothing… I don't know. I think I expected something a bit more… casual.

– You mean a pigsty. A guy living on his own…

She nodded. His place was not just clean, but clinical. The furniture was aligned precisely, each piece square with the next, square with the walls. There were no pictures, no books or CDs, not a magazine or a letter from the bank, no fliers from pizza parlours or the local fortune-teller. In his bathroom, a single tap stuck like a spike out from the wall above a square, stone basin. The tap worked automatically when you put your hands under it.

– I love the sofa, she said.

It was huge, a vast splash of maroon – the only colour in the flat – with no arms and a high, straight back. It faced the windows and occupied about half of the available space.

– It's a bit big for here.

She looked up at him, a question in her face.

– I used to live over there, he said, pointing out of the window at the flats on the opposite side of the narrow street, a warehouse block that, unlike Joe's, had once really been a warehouse. Its huge windows were lit and clear; many were open to the warm night air. Through one, they could see a woman moving slowly around her kitchen. She wore a black sleeveless top, and had short black hair. They watched while she made coffee. Joe wondered if she was alone, if she knew she was being watched. If she ever watched him.

– Why did you move?

– To get away, said Joe, and laughed. She waited. How much more was he going to have to give her?

– And there's the view, of course.

The woman in the opposite block had disappeared.

He asked if she'd like a glass of wine. She said she'd prefer coffee. From the barren kitchen area, he produced mugs, a coffeepot and boiling water; an ashtray.

– Right, she said. My turn.

No, thought Joe. Please no. He gestured at the empty flat with an unlit cigarette. You've not got a lot to go on.

– Oh, I don't know, you've given me plenty. Don't you want to hear about your early love life? Your sparkling career?

– No, said Joe. I really don't.

– We'll start at the beginning. When you lost your virginity.

– That could be messy.

– It was. You were in the ladies' toilets at your parents' pub.

– My parents owned a pub?

– Your dad did; at least, he ran it. The brewery owned it. Your mother never really approved.

– She wouldn't.

– You were fourteen.

He lit the cigarette, looked at the tip and said: I wish.

– Shut up, and let me tell it. You were fourteen. You used to slip down to the bar, to help your father out, when your mother thought you were doing your homework. He wouldn't let you serve the drinks, but you'd clear the glasses, empty the ashtrays. Your father would sit on a stool at the end of the bar, with a whisky and a cigar, telling jokes to the locals, abusing the bar staff. Some of the regulars would chat to you. They'd tease you, but you didn't say much. You just watched.

– Veronica was a regular, a blowsy, pudding-faced woman who pretended to flirt with you. You thought she was as old as the hills. But then she had her fortieth in the pub. She got paralytic and treated herself to a little present. She cornered you in the corridor, stuck her hand up your shirt, and her tongue in your mouth. It tasted of cigarettes and something sickly. She dragged you into the toilets. She wore leather trousers, and you thought her arse looked like the cushion on your mum's new sofa. It was over pretty quickly, and she was sick afterwards. You had to wash it out of your shirt. Your knees and elbows were all wet as well.

– Yuck.

– Indeed. But then we come to Alice.

– Was Alice nicer?

– Alice was terribly, terribly nice. You met at college and spent two years trying vaguely to get rid of her.

Joe said, At college? I didn't have sex again till then?

– I'm afraid not. There was a lot of mooning around looking wistful, a snog backstage at the school play and a few disco gropes, but nothing you could call sex. There wasn't a whole lot of sex with Alice either, come to that. And what there was, wasn't, let's say, especially adventurous. She was pretty, though, in a pale and droopy kind of way. You read 'Ode to a Nightingale' together and held hands as the sun came up over the Backs.

Joe smiled. I went to Cambridge?

— Yes. Your mother was delighted. Your father couldn't see the point and thought you'd turn out queer.

— I didn't, did I?

She laughed. Don't be silly. God kept you straight and narrow. Or maybe it was Alice. During the long vac she sent you letters on Womble notepaper: she thought it was funny, but it turned your stomach. You never said anything, though. The letters told you more than you wanted to know — about her parents and her part-time job, about the books she was reading for next term and how much she was missing you. Every time you saw Uncle Bulgaria lying on the doormat, waiting for you, you just knew you had to chuck her. But, somehow, it still took you a year to get around to it.

— In the end you worked yourself up to some self-righteous cruelty. She cried and said she couldn't believe that someone she loved could be so spiteful. You muttered that it was all your fault, and she shouldn't blame herself, which of course she did. You went off to play pool and get blind drunk.

Joe watched Lizzie finish her coffee. She stood up and began to drift around the flat, running her fingers along the straight edges, idly testing walls for hidden cupboard catches as she spoke. He stayed put, not relaxing into the sofa, but leaning forward with his elbows on his knees.

— You left Cambridge with a first and went on to… to what? What would have made your mother happy?

He shook his head. My mother didn't really do happy.

— Poor Joe. You moved to London to study law. Your mother was ecstatic; your father wondered if you were ever going to earn any money. You owed him quite a lot by then — the beer and fags and drugs weren't cheap — so this was something of a painful point. You made some friends at Law School, but less than you had lost from university.

She stopped wandering and turned to look at him. He dropped his face into his hands.

– You did your articles at a practice in the East End. The firm did a bit of everything – family, housing, crime – but mostly crime, which was what really turned you on. You thought you were a legal outlaw, pitting your wits against the forces of repression. You enjoyed the duty rotas, enjoyed being dragged from the pub or from your bed to spring some lowlife from the holding cells at Stoke Newington at two in the morning. Of all the stations you had to deal with, you liked Stokie and Brixton best. You loved the fact that people died in custody there. You were Henry Fonda; you were Ray Winstone, though it was mostly drunks and shoplifters you got to deal with. You made a few new friends at work, and lost those you still had from Law School.

Joe stood up and went to the window, turning his back on her. In the flat opposite, the woman in the black top was washing up. As she leant forward, a heavy crucifix swung out from between her breasts and dangled over the sink. He looked away, quickly.

Lizzie had followed him. She said, I haven't finished. She put her hands on his shoulders and tugged him back towards the sofa. She pushed him down, then sat beside him, looking past him to the window as she spoke: Then you met... Vanessa.

– Vanessa, he mumbled, not even making it a question.

– Vanessa: the improbably sexy French woman you met at Limehouse bailing out her boyfriend, who'd been caught with enough cocaine to count as intent to supply, and was going to jail, whatever you did. To your eyes she was perfect. She dressed in black and wore chunky silver jewellery she designed herself. She smoked Camels. When she spoke you could see the flash of a tongue stud in her mouth. Her accent made you feel stoned: happy, and with no desire to move, ever. She was into anal sex and bondage, though not with you, however much you wanted it.

Joe said, You don't... I've never...

But she didn't seem to hear.

– Pierre got four years and you were delighted. You took Vanessa home from court to comfort her. She cried in the taxi and you put your arm around her. She didn't push you away, and you thought life really couldn't get much better.

– During the appeal you visited all the time. Vanessa was friendly, pleased to see you. But the one time you tried to kiss her she laughed it off. She skipped away and invited you to a bar where she was going to meet some friends. You spent more time in Vanessa's flat than your own. You turned up in the morning to take her out for breakfast; you cooked for her friends; you gave her money for food, for rent, for drugs; you ignored all her hints and never left until she told you to.

Joe felt stifled, swamped. He tried to stand but Lizzie pushed him down again. She pulled him closer still, her lips brushing his ear as she spoke. His cigarette had burned itself out.

– Vanessa treated you like a pet. She'd sit in her underwear chatting to you while she painted her toenails, but never gave you any real reason to think she wanted sex with you. You didn't need a reason, though, did you? You're a man. And you were sure you were in love.

– One night you turned up early for a party. Vanessa was still getting ready. You helped her into a tight black dress, You brushed your hand against her buttocks, and were surprised by how small they felt. You fetched her favourite boots. You watched, a little nauseous, as she pushed studs into her lips, her nose and eyebrows. Her lipstick was maroon, thick and glossy as new-laid tarmac. She watched herself in the mirror, asked you how she looked. You stood behind her with your arms around her shoulders; you looked in the mirror, and said, 'Perfect,' as casually as you could.

Lizzie dropped her hand into his lap, and squeezed. He was hard: he couldn't help it. Then she stood up and began to drift around the flat again, never looking directly at him.

– After the party, you stayed on, her faithful puppy, until there were just you and Vanessa left, and a Dutchman who looked like a model. She said they had a little surprise for you. They led you to the bedroom. She stripped you down and told you to lie on the bed, arms and legs spread-eagled. You did, and they handcuffed your feet and hands to the metal bed frame.

Joe couldn't trust himself to open his mouth, or move.

– Then there, in front of you, around you, they did athletic, noisy things that Alice had never heard of, and you had only ever seen on the internet. At the end, she squatted over you, with the Dutchman behind her, thrusting professionally. Her face was inches from yours as she said, 'How do I look now, Joe?' and you said: 'Perfect.'

Joe ejaculated in his trousers. Shit. Was that what she wanted? He felt sticky, wet and miserable. He didn't care what she did. He wasn't going to say anything. She could do what she liked. He didn't care.

– It was Vanessa's leaving party. Pierre was inside and her money was gone, and so was most of yours, so she went home to Nantes. It was three days before the landlord came in to clear out the flat. He wasn't really surprised when it was knee-deep in party detritus. But he was none too pleased to find a delirious, semi-conscious naked man chained to a badly soiled bed. He did the decent thing, though, and got you to hospital. You were there three weeks recovering from the shock and dehydration. He brought grapes and demanded the six months' rent you thought you'd already paid, plus an astronomical cleaning bill. You coughed up and took on the lease. When you got out of hospital, you sold your flat and moved in here, to Vanessa's place.

Joe stood up at last.

– I'm sorry, he said. I've got to go to the bathroom.

She shouldn't talk like that, Joe thought. She shouldn't say those things. He had to change his clothes. He pulled a pair of jeans out of the laundry basket. They weren't clean, but they were better than the ones he had on.

She carried on, calling out from the living room:

– When you went back to work, they sacked you. You switched sides, and joined the CPS. You spent your life getting people sent to jail. When anybody asked, you said you thought most of them probably deserved it, but your heart was never really in it. After a while you just walked out. You sat here for a couple of months, ordering food off the internet, watching things shift on eBay for entertainment, never talking to anyone. When the money ran out you called a few old colleagues, got casual work doing police station duties at night and weekends. It suits you, working on and off when other people are having fun. It's a life, of sorts, and you're not unhappy.

– I'm not happy, either, said Joe.

She said, Who is?

## 4

They met again, of course. He rang her: Joe rang Lizzie. She answered, told him: Saturday morning. When he got to her place there was a *Time Out* on the table in the hall.

He said, Where are we going today?

– Covent Garden.

He grimaced. Do we have to? It'll be packed.

– There's nothing wrong with people, Joe.

On the bus she pressed against him, whispering lascivious French nonsense in his ear.

He said, Stop it, Lizzie; stop it.

They walked up through the market. She linked her arm through his. When they reached the corner of Floral Street, she pointed to the pub they'd been to the first time they met.

– In there, Joe. Wait for me at the bar. I won't be long.

Joe did as he was told. It was Saturday, but it was still early and the pub was fairly empty. At the bar he ordered a pint of lager and a large white wine. It was a different barmaid. He thought: Where do they get them all?

He turned to look back across the pub. Through the large plate window he could just make out Lizzie in the street outside. He watched as she approached a man, said something to him. He looked startled, then settled himself and said something back. Joe watched Lizzie laugh. They chatted for a moment; then they both turned to look at the pub. They walked towards it, and Joe turned back to face the bar.

He heard the scrape of chairs on the wooden floor as they found a table. He heard her say, 'No, I'll get them', and then felt her beside him at the bar.

– Lizzie, what are you doing?

– Smile, she said. Make it casual.

Joe turned, looked at the man she had brought in. He had wide-set eyes, a slightly upturned nose and no discernible chin. His ears were set at right angles to his head. He was fiddling with an unlit cigarette, turning it end over end and tapping it on the table. Joe grinned, his mouth flat. He waved, palm up, from the wrist. He was no one. Just a man in a bar.

He felt sick.

– Lizzie. Please? Why are you doing this?

– Helen, she said. My name is Helen.

– Helen, he said. Helen. I don't care. Mine is Joe.

– So is his.

– But mine *is*. It really is.

– It's just a name, she said. It doesn't matter.

She took the drinks she'd bought and carried them over to her table. The man said something to her, but she waved it away. He spoke again, pointing at the bar, at Joe. Helen turned to look at him, turned back; she shook her head.

Joe walked over to their table. The man stood up, bracing himself. He was a head shorter than Joe and maybe two stone heavier. Joe ignored him.

– Helen?

Helen smiled.

– Excuse me, she said. Do I know you?

# Staying Put

1

THE INTERIOR MINISTER shifted on the hard chair, clenching and settling his buttocks. He said, 'Have you started yet?'

The man must have heard his question, but he did not respond. The minister was not used to being ignored. This business of actually sitting for the artist was a recent innovation. In the past they had made do with photographs. This might be openness, and therefore correct, but he was not sure he approved: it meant dealing with artists. He shifted again. He could feel the weight of his hands on his knees, the pressure of his feet against the floor. They had only just begun, but it would be difficult, he thought, to remain still much longer. The artist was staring at him, at his face, but his hands made no move towards his easel. He didn't look much like an artist. For one thing, he was huge, with broad features and skin like raw meat. His hands were heavy and square: strong, like the paws of a tiger, the fingers thick and pale. He looked more like a peasant than a sculptor. When the minute detailing the arrangements crossed his desk, the minister had not recognised the name. His principal secretary said, 'He's the best we have, Minister.' The minister had been around a long time, and did not fail to detect the equivocation.

Finally, the artist began to draw, his hands moving quickly, but with a deftness and precision that belied their size. He stood back from the easel, a stick of charcoal in each hand, then approached it again, both arms swinging, his shoulders rolling, hands jabbing – right, right, left, right – like a boxer, the minister thought, like a street fighter, overwhelming his opponent with a flurry of blows.

Grin paused. The man was not much to look at, he'd have to say. Five foot six, five-seven, maybe, hair like cigarette ash – not just grey, but insubstantial, as though too strong a breeze might blow it away – no strength in him that Grin could see.

That couldn't be right. The man was in the ruling council after all, despite his father's history. That must have taken strength of a kind. He would have to look harder.

The minister asked if he were ambidextrous and Grin wished he would shut up. Eventually he said, 'Up to a point.'

'What does that mean?'

Grin began sketching again. Right – left – left.

'It means,' Grin said, watching his subject, 'that I masturbate with my right hand only.'

The minister laughed. Perhaps he was amused, Grin thought; probably he was not. The minister said, 'You will make the bust from your sketches?'

'No.'

That stopped him. 'Then...'

Grin tore the top sheet from the pad and let it drift to the floor. He said, 'I will make the bust from you. I draw...' – he attacked a second sheet – 'I draw to *see* you.'

'You don't see with your eyes?'

'I look with my eyes. I *see* with my hands.'

There. See what he could make of that.

The minister laughed again, more openly this time. 'Artists! Is that what they taught you at the Institute?'

Now Grin laughed, too. The Institute was uncertain terrain. A branch of the state, of course, but one that contained the sort of people and behaviour the state did not generally seek to accommodate. It had, he thought, done its best to teach him *not* to see. Shifting ground, he said, 'Drawing got me into the Institute. My parents had no connections, but my high school teacher wrote a letter of recommendation.'

The minister looked up at the ceiling for a moment, then back at Grin. 'He wrote that you drew like Raphael.'

Left – right. So the minister had read the letter. Grin knew that such hyperbole had been an act of bravado in itself. He said, 'You know that he was imprisoned?'

The minister nodded. 'But not for that.'

Grin continued working, preferring the soft scrape of charcoal to any voice. But the minister evidently wanted to talk. He said, 'So what *did* they teach you? At the Institute?'

Grin paused, let his huge hands fall to his sides. 'I learned that drawing was decadent. Self-indulgent. I embraced the machine-perfection of the camera.'

The minister smiled flatly. 'Bravo. Well said.'

But it was true. During his first eighteen months, Grin had taken, developed, printed and catalogued six thousand four hundred and seventeen black-and-white photographs of stones. In this he had not been encouraged; he had, however, been tolerated.

He continued staring, jabbing at the paper, staring again.

'Did you learn about self-indulgence from Abel Stark?'

Grin said, 'If I draw you enough I may know you.' Left – left – right. 'Your head. I will know your head.' Right – left. 'What is inside your head.'

That might shut him up.

The minister shifted on his chair again.

Grin ripped a second sheet from the pad.

The minister said, 'How is your friend Abel?'

Grin stepped to his left, putting the easel between him and the minister. A question about the Institute might – conceivably – have been mere conversation, an attempt to banish the silence of the unaccustomed situation. Possibly. Things might have changed that much. But a question about Abel? That could not be idle small talk. Or an attempt to elicit information, either. The minister would know more about Abel and his whereabouts than Grin – or anyone else – had done for several years now.

Grin said, 'What does your file tell you?'

'It tells me that you knew him.'

'Everyone knew him.'

That was true, at least. Abel had been hard to ignore. He was beautiful, for a start. The first time Grin saw him, he'd been implausibly dressed in a black suit, white shirt and a thin, bottle green tie. He had pointed up at Grin with a rolled umbrella, and said, as if to his companion: That's a lot of stones. Grin had been balancing uneasily atop a wooden stepladder, pinning a rigorous grid of flawless, almost identical photographs to a wall ten metres wide by four metres high. He said: six hundred and forty-eight; and Abel, through his nose, said: to be precise. Abel's companion, who wasn't beautiful, laughed. Grin said, why not be precise? The friend laughed again, higher and louder than was necessary. Abel did not laugh, though. He looked at the stones for a long time. Then he offered to help stick the remaining pictures to the wall; but Grin, suspecting satire, refused. When Abel turned to leave, Grin saw a large, six-pointed yellow star pinned to the back of his suit.

The minister said, 'The file tells me he was a sexual deviant.' He caught Grin's eye. 'That he had sex with boys as well as girls.'

'He liked to say that he was catholic. Universal.'

'Not Jewish?'

'Because of the star? You must know it wasn't always a star. Sometimes it was a hammer and sickle; sometimes a stars and stripes. Abel liked to provoke people. Like the Zazous, he used to say. Does your file tell you about the Zazous?'

When Grin asked about the star, Abel had insisted on buying more wine. They were in a tiny basement bar beneath a butcher's shop a long way from the Institute. The butcher's window rarely displayed much meat and Abel had passed the cellar door many times without ever realising it led anywhere of interest. At four in the afternoon the place had a dozen customers, and was full. There was no actual bar – just tables and mismatched chairs. An old woman Abel addressed as Auntie brought drinks from another room which Grin could only glimpse through a doorway as she backed through a curtain of thin metal chains, a glass in each hand. The wine was filthy – domestic, almost black and with a chemical taste that reminded Grin of paint thinner – but at least it was wine, Abel said. Not vodka.

'In Paris,' Abel said, 'during the German occupation, the Zazous dressed as young dandies. Imagine! They wore immaculate suits, straw hats, canes. They loved jazz and shocking people. Some of them wore the yellow star, though very few were Jewish. They did it mostly to annoy.' He paused. 'And they succeeded. The Zazous had no politics.'

'And you?' Grin asked.

Abel refilled their glasses. 'I am living history. Did you know that here, in our own home town, we had the Mr Johnsons?'

Grin had never heard of them.

'Just after the war. They were a bit like the Zazous, although there weren't as many of them. And they were probably a lot less stylish. But they wore the best suits they could, dark glasses, and carried furled umbrellas. There are a few people you wouldn't guess – big people, now – who had a youthful fling with the Mr Johnsons. The name came from a '40s blues singer who used to growl at his pianist: *Please Mr Johnson, don't play the blues so sad.* They lasted exactly one summer.'

The minister said, 'Actually, it wasn't the star. I was thinking more of his circumcised cock. Or of what he liked to do with it.'

Grin said nothing.

'You, of course, refused his disgusting advances. Your partnership was purely artistic.'

Grin could not be mistaken now: these were not questions. Neither were they facts. They were weapons.

He tugged a third sheet from the pad. He said, 'I think we should not carry on. The light is not good.'

It was June and the sun would not set for several hours. But, outside, heavy grey clouds had muddied a once-bright afternoon. The air seemed thick with rain. Even the high ceilings and tall windows of the Ministry of the Interior could not prevent the gloom from pooling and settling around them.

Grin picked the first sheets from the floor. Each bore four or five sketches – heads, hands, ears, a disembodied nose. None, he thought, yet made sense of a man – small, soft, weak-eyed – capable of exercising such unrestricted power.

The minister rose, held out his hand. 'May I see them?'

'Of course.'

He glanced over the sketches, nodding, apparently in appreciation. 'Good,' he said. 'I like that.' He was pointing at the nose, smiling. 'Do you know Gogol?'

Again, Grin assumed that the minister was not merely making conversation. Gogol was acceptable – streets still bore his name – but his original memorial in Moscow had been replaced with a Socialist Realist statue in the 1950s. Grin said yes, he knew Gogol, hoping that nothing more was expected.

The minister handed back the sketches. 'How much longer will it take you?'

It was hard to say.

The minister crossed the vast space towards his desk, the rubber soles of his shoes squeaking lightly on the parquet floor. He pressed a button. 'We will begin again on Tuesday.'

It made no difference to Grin, who had no other work, but he said, 'Tuesday might be difficult, Minister.'

The minister was having none of it. 'A car will pick you up at noon.'

2

The car arrived punctually. Grin stood on the pavement with his easel and satchel, waiting for the driver to get out and open the boot. When it was obvious that he would not move, Grin attempted to open the boot himself, whereupon the driver, a round man with no neck and diamond-shaped gaps between the buttons of his shirt where it stretched across his belly, was out in the road at once, shouting. What did Grin think he was doing? Grin explained, and the driver said, 'This is a government car!'

'And I have to take my easel to the Ministry.'

'Nobody said there was an easel.'

'Nevertheless,' said Grin, 'here it is.'

The boot was full, apparently; Grin knew better than to ask with what. He said he could prop the easel against the back seats while he sat in the front, but the driver would not hear of it. This was a government car: passengers sat in the back.

Grin asked the driver to wait, and carried the easel back up two flights of stairs to the apartment he shared with Kirsten. When he returned the driver offered to put his satchel in the boot.

The minister said, 'You're late.' Something about his manner – perhaps the way he rose from his desk as he spoke, gesturing towards the chair placed alone in the middle of the vast office – gave Grin the impression that the minister's impatience was more formal than real, part of a game.

'I apologise, Minister.'

That seemed to rouse his suspicion. 'I expect that fool of a driver was late? Or drunk?'

The delay was not entirely due to the argument about the easel. In the last few days the road seemed to have acquired a couple of additional checkpoints. Arriving at the Ministry, Grin had been put through all the usual security procedures – his name taken, his ID checked, a visitor's pass made up, his bag searched – but this time the guard had actually looked into the bag. He had held up two sticks of charcoal and asked Grin what they were.

Grin said, 'The driver was quite punctual. And sober, as far as I could tell.'

The minister laughed. 'Now I know you're lying.' He watched Grin closely, smiling. 'Don't worry, we don't shoot people any more.'

He sat on the hard chair, put his hands on his knees, and said, 'To work!'

Grin picked up a second chair from against a wall and set it down opposite the minister's. The minister said, 'You have no easel today?'

'No. Not today.'

'You will begin the bust?'

'No. Today I will make more sketches.'

He took a sketchpad and charcoal from his satchel, balanced the pad on one knee and stared at the minister's head. Where was the power? The strength he must possess to do the things he had done? To survive this long? Grin knew – everybody knew – that the minister's father had been a partisan in the war, had helped to liberate the country, helped lead it in the early days. But he had been a liberal and his career had not survived the change; his own son's denunciation of his crimes had provided the final impetus for his defection. The son had flourished. Now, under the ash grey hair, his head was heavy, with high cheekbones and sagging jowls: together they made great slabs of his cheeks. The ears had large, fleshy lobes, the nose was thick, the nostrils bulging either side. It was the head of a much larger man. Perhaps that was where he could start? His way in.

He began to draw. An imaginary view, as if from above, with exaggerated perspective. The minister's cheeks became cliff faces, his body dwindling away to nothing. Not right, not yet. Balancing the pad on his knees made it hard to use both hands. It slipped and fell to the floor between them. Grin saw the minister looking at his distorted portrait, saw its inadequacy through the other man's eyes – it now looked no more than a cheap caricature – and hastened to pick it up. As he straightened up he found himself close to the minister and looking into his eyes. They were set deep in their sockets, half-covered by heavy lids, the way he had drawn them in the previous session, but where before he had thought them weak, he now saw that they were black, that there was no sheen to them, as if they took in light, took in everything, and gave nothing back.

That was where he would have to start.

He tore up the first sketch and began again. They were silent, with just the soft scratch of charcoal on heavy paper between them. After a while, the minister said, 'Do you know what Abel's father says about you?'

Grin said, 'I can imagine.'

'He says you corrupted his son. He says you dragged him down into a world of perverts and anti-social elements. That you stole his girlfriend. He is disgusted that you have the gall to pretend to live like a normal man. What do you say to that?'

Grin said, 'Perhaps he should ask himself how his son got into the Institute in the first place.'

The minister smiled enough to show the points of his teeth. 'And, if he asked you instead, what would you say?'

Grin said nothing.

'Would you tell him that his son sucked off the deputy director of the Institute of Design, and then sold that information to the chief of police? Is that what you would say?'

Perhaps. That was what Abel had told him, after all, in the bar beneath the meat-less butcher's shop.

'What do you want me to say, Minister?'

'Whatever you like. We're just passing the time here.'

Grin shook his head. When had either of them ever said whatever they liked? He said, 'You know what I told them. It's in your files.' The minister would know what he had said to the Institute's director, and he would know why he had said it. He would know about his mother's illness, and the treatment it had needed. It would all be in the files. There was no point in repeating it now.

When the minister spoke again, he only seemed to change tack. He said, 'Peregrine is an unusual name.'

Grin did not respond.

'Let us see if I can picture the parents who would call their son Peregrine.' The minister closed his eyes. 'I see them in jackets with patched elbows, serving potato cakes on cracked Meissen plates that had belonged to your great-grandparents; I see them, playing piano quite badly on Sundays.'

Grin said, 'Could you keep your eyes open, please?'

The minister opened his eyes again, looked directly at Grin. 'They did not stand out. Your father once made a joke that three of his students reported to their supervisor, but it was not serious; he kept his job. And yet he called you Peregrine?'

Grin did not respond. The minister said, 'Peregrine was a wanderer, no? But you have stayed put?'

The phrase was no more innocent than any of the minister's conversation. It was true – obvious – that Grin had stayed, had not left when others had done so. (Abel had not left. He had disappeared. There was a difference.)

Grin said, 'Peregrine is also the patron saint of cancer sufferers. My real father died while my mother was pregnant. They had planned a wedding, but he was diagnosed with pancreatic cancer. Within a month – before they could marry – he was dead. But my mother is a resourceful woman. There was a single man on the staff of the school where she taught. The wedding went ahead.'

The minister nodded appreciatively. 'And she named her son after the saint who had failed her?'

Grin tore off a page and began a new sketch. Unlike his father, his mother's cancer had been successfully treated.

The minister said, 'Is any of that true?'

'Is it not in my file?'

The minister shook his head.

'Then it can't be true,' said Grin. 'Can it?'

The minister roared with laughter. 'Good for you, Peregrine Berg. I like you. I'm glad they sent you to me.'

'You didn't choose me?'

The minister shook his head again, and smiled. 'There are limits, Grin, to the power of a middle-ranking minister. Some things are beyond even me.'

Grin continued sketching until, after twenty or thirty minutes of more comfortable silence, there was a knock at the door and the principal secretary entered the room.

'Excuse me, Minister.'

The minister did not stand up. 'What is it?'

'Perhaps it would be better...'

The minister turned back to Grin. 'He wants you to leave. Do you want to leave?'

'It would be better, Minister,' said the secretary. 'I have had a reply from the trade union secretariat. They have agreed to meet you at two. There will be a demonstration. It is authorised, but we must make arrangements.'

Grin said, 'I can leave.' He stood up.

Sighing, the minister stood up, too. 'Next time,' he said, 'you can start on the bust?'

Grin said, 'Next time, yes.'

'I'll look forward to it.'

### 3

When Grin said the bags of wet clay had to go in the boot, the driver made no objection. In the minister's office, the chair stood in the middle of a vast tarpaulin, placed there to protect the parquet. The minister greeted him warmly, making no mention of the delay that the driver's intricate route, and the still more thorough security inspections, had occasioned. 'Good morning, Berg. Today we make the bust, no?'

'No, Minister.'

'No?'

'Today, if we are lucky, I will make a model of the bust. If you like the model, and the committee approves, I will begin to make the bust.'

The minister seemed to shrink slightly. 'You are very... painstaking. Do you always go to all this trouble?'

Pain? Trouble? It meant nothing. 'Always, Minister.'

The minister laughed, and sat down. 'If it can't be helped, we might as well get on.'

Grin set up a small, stained folding table, opened one of

the bags of clay and slapped it down with a wet smack. He began to shape a smooth ball, an egg, then a rectangular block. He set the egg upon the block – head and shoulders – then opened a second bag and began pulling thumb-sized lumps, layering them upon the egg and the block, building them up.

'Do you know how you received this commission, Grin?'

'No.' He did not want to know. He wanted it done. Done properly, though: precisely; even now.

'Did you ask? When you were summoned to the Ministry of Culture, did you say, why me?'

'Of course not.'

'Of course not. You are no fool. I asked, though. Last week, after you left. I had someone find out for me. And do you know? It's your girlfriend you have to thank.'

Would he never stop digging away like this? Grin thought he had passed this test last time. 'She is not my girlfriend.'

'Nonetheless, I am told she approached the former director of your Institute. She was looking for a project, for you. She was worried about you, Grin. All those stones.'

There was a knock at the door. A young civil servant entered the room and paused, apparently unnerved by the sight. He crossed the tarpaulin and whispered to the Minister, his back towards Grin.

Grin heard the minister sigh and say, 'Of course not.' The civil servant left.

When Abel disappeared, Grin had done nothing, made nothing, for several months. He told Kirsten he was waiting for Abel to return. Then, to while away the time, he had bought new tools and begun to carve. Plaster first; then wood. The work was primitive to begin with, crude, but vigorous; of a plebeian energy the official galleries loved, but which, over the years, he had gradually tamed. His carvings became smaller, more intricate and exquisite. He made figures – animals and birds – which reminded Kirsten of classical

Japanese art. She warned him they would bring renewed whispers of decadence, of aestheticism. Slowly, the carvings became smaller still: smoother, rounder, more tactile and, it seemed, less figurative, until eventually Kirsten realised he was carving pebbles. Perfect, weather-worn, sea-ground *wooden* pebbles. He carved hundreds of them, thousands – six thousand four hundred and seventeen. And then he stopped. Abel would not return.

Layer by layer, Grin built up the cheekbones, the brow. How could he recreate those black eyes?

The minister said, 'The director is retired now, of course, but still connected. He said that he would see what he could do.'

Grin understood. 'And here I am.'

The minister laughed. 'And here you are. And how are you getting on?'

'There is still a lot to do. Please keep still, Minister.'

'Don't call me that, Grin. These people...' – he gestured towards the door – 'secretaries, assistant secretaries, principal assistant secretaries: they call me Minister. I wasn't born a politician, you know.'

Grin said, 'Please.'

'Have you heard of the Mr Johnsons, Grin? Would you believe I was a Mr Johnson once? Just after the war, when my father was a minister.'

We can't be friends, Grin thought. Just because I stood up to you and made you laugh. It was not safe.

'You will know that I denounced my father, Grin. But he was a weak man, for all his heroic reputation. He did not see things through.'

Would he never stop talking?

'For what it's worth, it did my father no harm. I gave them nothing they didn't have already, beyond the fact of my saying it. But that's the point, isn't it?'

Grin understood: betrayal was the point, not information.

The minister said, 'It's never about the one denounced,

is it? Never. You understand that, don't you?'

They knew. They'd always known. Abel would have disappeared anyway. He didn't believe it, but he understood: of course he did. Again, the light was failing; heavy summer thunderclouds clogged the air.

'So I joined the Youth League. But what of it? We had a new society to build. I had been a Mr Johnson and I had been arrested, I had no choice. Just like you. There: we have more in common than you might suppose. But I cannot say I wouldn't have made the same decision if I'd had a choice.' He paused. 'What was it Brecht said? It is still not given to us not to kill. Some people seem to think they can change society without themselves changing. There are things I have done that I am proud of. Others... not so proud. But I have done them. I will not pretend I haven't.'

He would not pretend. Grin knew he could finish now. He fashioned an ear, using a blunt wooden spatula to create the delicate internal whorl.

'In Berlin they no longer have a wall. In Russia that fool Yeltsin sits drunk upon a tank to save democracy. But it is weakness, Grin, to walk away from responsibility. I am staying put. We have not yet done what we set out to do.'

The minister fell silent. Grin fashioned a second ear. He would work up to the eyes, now. Now that he knew.

Grin wiped clay from his hands. The minister stretched and said, 'I am tired.'

They both looked at the model taking shape before them. Grin said, 'It is a start.'

The minister said, 'It is.' He stood up, walked over to Grin's table and examined the half-formed bust more closely. 'It's nearly finished.'

Grin disagreed, but the minister waved away his objections. He said, 'Of course, my father may outlive me yet. I hear that he is not well. Cancer of the mouth.' He turned to Grin. 'But you never know. They say that the treatment he gets in England is almost as good as ours.' He laughed loudly then.

4

The statues were due to be unveiled at the anniversary celebrations. Each had been cast on an heroic scale, mounted on a plinth in the capital's main square, facing the government offices, then wrapped in hectares of opaque white plastic, taped down like fragile parcels.

On the morning of the celebration, however, as people began to gather in the square at dawn, they found that someone had already cut away the plastic sheeting and prised off the brass name plaques. Thirteen statues ringed the square, exposed, their bronze eyes not staring down at those below, but gazing blindly over their heads, towards the government building where, later that morning, their real-life counterparts would gather and prepare to meet their fellow citizens.

Grin was among the first to arrive in the square. He watched the crowd gather and take stock of the exposed statuary. The bust of the Leader was obvious – larger than any of the others, and placed dead centre, directly opposite the balcony from which the real Leader would soon make his address, six ministers arranged on either side. As the crowd thickened, Grin saw people elbow their way through from one statue to another, laughing, guessing, joking, pointing. He leaned against the plinth beneath his bust of the minister of the interior, hands in the pockets of his jacket. He watched people stare up at its face, at its eyes; they looked troubled, as if it reminded them of somebody, but they were not sure who. He saw two young men in jeans and heavy metal t-shirts point up at it and pause, a joke dying on the lips of one. 'Who gives a shit?' he heard the other say. 'Those pricks are all the same.'

As the press of bodies thickened, the interior minister's principal secretary became concerned. By nine o'clock there were already more people than had been authorised or arranged, and yet more were arriving all the time, crowding into the square and the surrounding streets, swarming up the lampposts and the walls and window sills of government buildings without restraint or respect. The noise of so many people talking, shouting, laughing – simply *being* – was hard to ignore. It became a throb, a pulse, a heart-beat, constant as life. The minister told him not to be such an old hen.

The Leader would address the crowd at eleven, with the ruling council lined up behind him on the balcony. When he sat down – sometime in the early afternoon – the statues were to have been unveiled. But they were uncovered already. What should they do now, the principal secretary asked, to signal the end of the official ceremony? The minister said he doubted there would be a problem. They would know.

At a quarter to eleven the members of the ruling council assembled in an anteroom. Over the crowd's muffled thrum they teased each other about the quality of their representations. The defence minister said his grandson could have done a better job.

Unseen by his colleagues, the interior minister took off his watch and dropped it, together with his cell phone and his wallet, into an eighteenth-century porcelain fruit bowl that sat on an occasional table against the rear wall of the room. He took his place by the door to the balcony.

Outside, the immense crowd fell silent.

# Cities From a Train

FOR VICTOR, THE end began when he read in a local paper the story of a man who had attempted – and failed – to run a marathon backwards. The runner had been trying to raise funds for research into a rare neurological disease, which causes sufferers gradually to regress, unlearning step-by-step all the skills they have amassed during their lifetime. Unlike more common forms of dementia, he read, it is not memories that are lost but the ability to interpret them, along with the acquired motor skills, making it progressively more difficult to function effectively, then independently, then finally to walk or stand at all until the victim is left mewling and puking like an infant. At this point the disease appears to resolve spontaneously, allowing or requiring the patient to begin all over again the business of life, to relearn the physical and theoretical skills needed to make sense of the innumerable memories still crowding his or her brain. Confronted by the enormity, the terror and – Victor imagined – the futility of the task, the majority of patients become depressed or delusional, and recovery is rarely complete.

He had found the newspaper on his seat. It was a local freesheet from a small city through which his train would pass, but which he believed he had never visited. At first, he had simply moved it to the vacant place next to his in the hope that it might discourage anyone else from sitting there.

He had not been on a train – a proper train, he thought, with toilets and a buffet car, a train that carved through fields, leaving one town before it reached the next instead of merely halting from suburb to suburb as if following a string of sausages – for as long as he could remember. This one seemed familiar enough at first, though: crowded, cramped, his seat comfortable but facing backwards – his back to the engine

– a little plastic tray folding down into his lap from the rear of the seat in front. Or the front of the seat behind, he supposed, from the train's point of view, or from that of an observer on the platform, had there been anyone to watch him leave. He balanced a paper coffee cup on the tray, then had to grab it quickly when the child in front of him – a child of about Lily's age – braced her feet against the seat in front of *her* and launched herself backwards, or forwards, towards Victor. When the train pulled out, Victor watched the metropolis slide out of view, the wreckage piling up behind him, propelling him full-tilt before an ever-burgeoning past. All this was familiar.

There was something wrong, however; or something not quite right, at least. It tugged at Victor, abrading his nerves. He tried to skewer the source of his unease, but could not, and turned to the abandoned newspaper for distraction. Then, approaching a satellite town, the train rattled across the points and Victor realised that the problem was not real, not a carcass he could lay out on the block, but an absence, a hole where something should have been. There was a constant sucking sound, but no clicking from the rails, none of the familiar diggety-dig, diggety-dig that had characterised all the trains in all the stories he had told Lily every day for what now seemed a another lifetime. It was progress, he supposed; but without that rhythmic clatter it would be hard to attain the state of hypnotic suspension that he'd always regarded as the best feature of long train journeys. To travel vacantly was, to Victor's mind, a better thing than to arrive.

Certainly better than to arrive today. He pictured his sister Freddie waiting for him at the station: a study of rude, bovine health, her over-large hands skulking in her armpits or beating each other for warmth, the woollen flaps of her inane Tibetan hat jogging like the ears of an excited spaniel as she stomped forward to crush him to her solid, creaturely udders. She'd make some comment about how he seemed to have lost weight, how there was nothing to him now. It would be just as if their mother hadn't died at all. Freddie would drive him home, to the house, in a battered, anonymous car that she'd have given a name culled from a favourite children's book or TV programme, or from her half-baked readings of Chinese philosophy. She would invite him to guess the name, and would refuse to be put off by his deliberately obtuse responses – Myra, after Hindley, perhaps? Hirohito? Or: Victor? You named it after me? At last she'd laugh and slap him on the shoulder and say something like, no, silly, it's Muttley. Didn't you hear that chugging laugh when I started him up? Isn't that perfect? And then, at that moment, he would remember that she had christened a previous car Violet Elizabeth after the tooth-shattering scream it let out whenever she engaged second gear. And he would agree that, yes, Muttley was perfect. They'd be silent for a while, listening to the noise of the engine, and then she would turn to look at him and say something like, But seriously, Victor, how have you been?

And he'd say something non-committal, like, Oh, you know.

And she'd say, Yeah, I guess we never knew how much we took her for granted. How much we loved her.

And he'd think, but not say: Speak for yourself.

Then they would arrive and his father would be in the wrong half of the house for the first time in – what? – twenty-five years? He'd be in her half, downstairs, in the living room – her bedroom – playing the paterfamilias, welcoming relatives and pointing them towards the flimsy reed coffin parked squarely on the bed, or towards the table where there'd be cans of lager and glasses of sherry and peanuts still in their foil packets for later, for the guests, the mourners, to help themselves, he'd say, when they came back afterwards. His father would ask how he was, perhaps even ask how Sara was, and the little one. He wouldn't remember his granddaughter's name, and Victor would stop to wonder whether he had, in fact, ever told him it was Lily, and would think there didn't seem to be much point now.

His father would introduce him to the man from the

Humanist Society he'd found on the internet, who was going to lead the celebration. The humanist would never have met Victor's mother, who'd been a Catholic, attending Mass and regularly confessing whatever middling sins she had managed to accumulate: mostly anger, Victor supposed. She had christened neither of her children, thanks to their father's objections, but she had cooked fish every Friday; she had left some on the stairs for Victor's father to take up and eat in his half of the house, alone, and had done so even after he announced through Freddie that he had become a vegetarian. His father had declared his vegetarianism, he now recalled, just when Victor told him he was going to be a butcher. Or perhaps it was the other way around? Freddie, the diplomat, had described for them both the famous (she said) Taoist figure of the butcher who had carved oxen with the grace of a dancer. The point was not *what* one did, she said, but *how* one approached the task; provided that one brought no extrinsic purpose to it, any action could be holy.

Victor would shake hands with a sprinkling of distant, dimly remembered relatives and would be unable to recall the last time they had met. He would try to evade their polite questions about Sara and Lily and their life together in the metropolis, about business, about the shop. He'd mutter something about trade being tough these days; he would not explain why his wife and daughter were not there. He would fail to ask any questions in return, and the conversations would expire gracelessly.

There would be no line of beetle-black Daimlers blocking the narrow road outside the house. No: they would drive out to a freezing, wind-whipped hillside in a haphazard congeries of vehicles, Victor once again beside his sister in Muttley, their mother in the back of their father's van, boxed up for delivery to her last, inevitable indignity. Perhaps in another lifetime the cemetery might grow to fit the sylvan promise of a woodland burial; but for now, Victor foresaw, it would remind him of nothing so much as archive footage from the first World War, the sky dark and wet, the ground ripped open to black mud, through which they would pass with jerky, unnatural movements, all sound sucked away.

He did not know exactly how his father would seek the final say in the violent, soundless war that had waged for three decades, but he knew the opportunity would not be missed. His father would impose himself, make his mark; it would be naive of Victor to imagine that he might exercise restraint. After all, Victor asked himself: would he? When the time came, would he act any differently?

Only when the train pulled out of a station did Victor realise that it had even stopped. He watched the city recede as they beat through fields of lumpy, fibrous vegetables that gave off the odour of wet towels. As the train gathered speed, he returned to the paper and found that it was local to the city they had just left. It was not a place he had ever visited, he thought, or probably ever would, but it must contain its own share of misery and absurdity: the story of the marathon runner's perverse attempt to ameliorate the impact of his father's brain disease seemed to promise as much.

It had evidently been a slow news week; the journalist had been afforded ample space to provide colour and detail. The onset of the disease is gradual, Victor read, but it accelerates dramatically as the sufferer re-approaches those stages of life when he or she had learned the most. The runner's father, for example – a retired master butcher whose shop was known and treasured in the town, but which the runner had not chosen to take over – had at first noticed only that his golf was deteriorating, that the slice he'd finally cured after retirement had returned, sending balls flying into the lake at the sixth. Then one Sunday, carving a perfect rib joint, he noticed that, while he was sure his son was a great disappointment to him, he could no longer recall precisely why. Later, Victor read, the same became true of his wife, who had died some years earlier for reasons the butcher could no longer bring to mind. After a while, however, his family ceased to disappoint him altogether and became, momentarily, a source of intense satisfaction, and even joy. All this he had told his son innocently, step by step, with an increasingly child-like wonder at a curious world.

There followed a brief but traumatic period during which the butcher lost all knowledge of cuts and cooking times and hanging periods, and of the use and maintenance of knives: knowing they were sharp, could slice meat and should be handled with care did not prevent him cutting the tip off his tongue while eating pasta. He lost the thumb and two fingers of his left hand attempting to make sausages out of his granddaughter's pet rabbits. (As he read this, the scars on Victor's own hands seemed to throb.) In hospital the scale of the butcher's problems became apparent and diagnosis possible at about the same time as his ability to understand the implications disappeared forever.

The runner was described as an athlete, a vegetarian and a former life coach. He had run for eleven hours fifty-six before collapsing in agony at the twenty-second mile. The runner's wife was said to be very proud of what he had done for his father, although the resulting damage to both Achilles' tendons was certain to affect his future performance, his career and sponsorship potential, and so threaten the security of their young family.

Victor told Freddie about the story as they crawled out of the station in *Wu-wei*. (Named after the Taoist slogan of 'non-purposive action', which she said described the car's un-businesslike approach to the business of transportation). She said they'd been there, to that city, as children: did he remember?

Victor didn't.

Their father had taken them on a mystery trip, she said, back when he was still speaking to Mum. They'd all gone to the bus station and boarded the first coach that left: that was where they'd ended up.

Victor remembered the trip but said it was to somewhere else, that their mother hadn't come because it had been a

Sunday morning. He wanted Freddie to be wrong. He wanted her to talk about the 'former life coach'. He wanted to tease her, to ask if one could retrospectively improve one's past lives, and thereby increase the karma one brought to one's present incarnation.

They pulled up outside the house. Freddie said, 'Go easy on Dad, Victor. You might find he's acting a little strangely.'

Victor said, 'No change there, then.'

'Really. Despite everything, he's taken this very hard.'

'So hard he's going to bury her under a tree?'

'What?'

'With a few feeble mumblings from a total stranger?'

Freddie looked at Victor for a long time.

'What's happened, Victor? Has something happened with Sara?'

'Oh, you know,' said Victor.

Freddie didn't and Victor didn't say. Eventually she gave up.

'You'll be nice to Fr Calley, too, won't you?'

'Will he even be there?'

'I should think so,' Freddie said. 'He's saying the Mass.'


The churchyard was cold, but sheltered from the wind. The mound of earth beside the grave had been neatly turfed. Fr Calley spoke of both the challenges and the rewards of a lifetime's love. That's how it was with God, he said.

Afterwards, during the wake – which was large and, for the most part, good-humoured – Victor's father said in the end it didn't matter what he believed. He said each day was another chance to get things right.

Victor sought out Freddie and asked her to drive him back to the station.

'What are you going to do?' she said. 'When you get home?'

'I'm not going home.'

'Then where?'

'There's a place, a city. About halfway back from here. I

told you about it this morning.'

Freddie opened her mouth to speak, but Victor screwed up his eyes and pinched his lips together with his fingers. It was something they had done as children. She smiled, and they embraced. 'Take care,' she said.

Victor held up both hands, palms outwards, fingertips spread. There were more scars than he could remember, but all ten digits remained.

'I always have,' he said.

# Hostage

*I knew you once: but in Paradise,*
*If we meet, I will pass nor turn my face.*
- Robert Browning

1

ALL THE WAY home she had the feeling something wasn't right. It was late, but not too late for the last train, and dark on the walk from the station – but what would she expect? Autumn had almost collapsed into winter: the last leaves huddled around streetlights like pickets at a brazier, throwing the pavements into irregular, shifting shadow. She was drunk, of course, but that wasn't it. Outside the station the road works that had been there in the morning, that had been there for weeks, weren't there. The corner shop was closed, its windows shuttered and blank. It was after midnight... of course it was shut. She was just drunk.

The team had been out after work, because it was Thursday and the markets had been up and down, but mostly because it was Thursday. She and Shazia had downed a couple of margaritas before someone started in on pitchers of sangria. When the lights came on – bright, scouring lights that showed up all your pores – the bouncers held the doors open, letting cold November air do their work for them. They said, Haven't you got homes to go to? Yes, she thought, she had.

So: she was drunk – drunker than she probably ought to be at her age, on a Thursday; drunk enough to fall asleep on the train. Ordinary drunk, then – not paralytic, not like she couldn't walk; and anyway, it wasn't that. It was just something floating in the corner of her eye. Something tugging at her like a detail in a thriller she knew must be a clue if she could only work out why. Sometimes, she'd try to puzzle them out while she read, but mostly she would just plough on, knowing it made no difference, knowing it would work itself out anyway.

The back door was unlocked, the way he left it when she was out late. She dropped her case in the kitchen, by the table; in the dark she could just make out a small pile of keys, a mobile and a couple of letters, one from the bank.

She climbed the stairs. Rob had rolled over to her side of the bed. She tipped him back as far as she dared and slipped in beside him. He rolled again and curled his arm around her, kissed the back of her neck, but she knew he was still asleep. She peeled him off and shoved him onto his back, hoping he wouldn't snore.

When she woke, his side of the bed was warm, but he wasn't there. Then he *was* there, at the window, cracking open the blinds on a drear, grey winter's morning, saying brightly: 'Another day in paradise.'

She curled herself tighter and pulled the sheet over her head. He said, 'Don't let your coffee get cold. Love you.' Then he left.

She thought she heard other voices – high, light, insubstantial – before the front door closed and a car engine coughed into life outside. She pushed back the sheet. She must be late. The grey November light was bright enough to pin shut her eyes. She opened them again more slowly.

The blond IKEA wardrobe with the loose hinge was on the wrong side of the room. It should have been on the left, in the alcove between the fireplace and the bay window instead of on the right. She got out of bed, supporting her head with her hands, and opened the wardrobe door. The clothes were not hers. They were *like* hers: the labels and the styles seemed familiar, but familiar like memories, not like daily life. The shoes were mostly flats and there was no sign of the silk and mohair suit she usually wore to shore up a hangover. She picked something equally expensive but functional, and headed downstairs to the kitchen, where she found a table with three dirty bowls and glasses and, clasped to the fridge by a hinged magnetic frog, a photograph of a man being hugged by two identical girls, all tangles of dark shiny hair blown across perfect adolescent skin, upon whom she knew, with a sudden, cold-eyed sobriety beyond all doubt, she had never in her life set eyes before.

2

He had read, or heard – he could not now be sure which, or when; but the dictum had stuck in his head because it had seemed so extravagantly untrue – that all relationships are power relationships, that one partner always holds more power than the other, and that the power depends on the weakness of the other, on which of them needs the other more; no equilibrium is ever reached.

A few years later, it had seemed to him true; it seemed to him, furthermore, that *he* had the power; that, of the two of them, it was she who needed him, he who could, if it came to it, just walk away.

Then they had the girls – twins – and everything became harder. Harder to stay; harder even to imagine leaving, until one day – the girls would have been nine – he had watched Aimee screw up her eyes and push the plunger on the hypodermic in her diabetic mother's thigh while Nicole looked on, her face a perfect blend of fascination and disgust, and he realised quite suddenly, without having thought of it for years, that he no longer had the power, that the woman he thought he had chosen to love had acquired reinforcements. It was now unthinkable for him to live without her strength, much less abandon it of his own accord. And then she disappeared.

3

Shazia, pressing her hand over the mouthpiece of her telephone, said: 'You're late.'

'It's a long story.'

Shazia grinned. 'I saw the first four acts.' She widened her eyes, expecting gossip. But, as Ines dumped her bag and slumped into her chair, a tropical-grade shit-storm broke over the world of traded reinsurance and for the next seven hours neither she nor Shazia had time to talk. A tidal wave of greed and fear rushed west towards them, gathering pace as one by one the eastern markets closed, until the wave broke, somewhere over Amsterdam and they were done and could leave the Yanks to wipe up the mess. They reckoned they were maybe just the tiniest fraction of a point ahead. But at least they hadn't lost, and it was the weekend.

They were waiting for four Bloody Marys – it saved time queuing – when Shazia demanded details. 'You weren't sick on the tube?'

Ines told her some of it, while Shazia listened, open-mouthed. 'This happened? This isn't something you daydreamed on the way in?'

Ines shook her head.

'Really?'

'Really.' Ines paid for the drinks and they shoved their way to a corner where there was a shelf large enough to put their glasses down.

Shazia said, 'You must have realised? I mean, come on.'

Ines thought about the picture of the man with the two girls. But she wasn't going to mention that, not even to Shazia. Instead she said that as she left the house that morning – a between-the-wars semi like her own, but with a gate on the right hand side of the garden, not the left – as soon as she began walking to the tube, it was obvious what had happened. She'd just turned the wrong way.

Shazia said, 'Well that explains everything.'

'Last night. At Bank, you know?' Ines said. 'Where you go down the escalator, and then back on yourself and down again, and then turn right for northbound and left for south, or whichever way it is. I do it every day and I still couldn't say for sure. I just don't look. But, whatever, I must have turned the wrong way. By the time I got to the station this morning I was sure it was going to be Morden, Collier's Wood, something like that.'

'And was it?'

'South Wimbledon.'

'Class.' Shazia lived in Clerkenwell; Ines somewhere further north than Shazia said she'd ever been, somewhere just below the M25.

They finished their first drinks, started the second. When it looked like Ines wasn't going to say anything more, Shazia said, 'Was he cute?'

Ines honestly didn't know: she hadn't looked.

'So he could be?'

'That's not the point.'

'It's always the point. If he's cute, you could have this whole secret life thing going on. How exciting is that? You could just disappear into the fantasy world of... South Wimbledon.' Shazia's straight face cracked. Choking on laughter and vodka she pointed at Ines: 'Your face!'

'I don't want to disappear. I don't want a new start. That's what men do.'

Shazia sighed. 'Men, right.'

'Right. Men rip everything up and start again when they can't cope with what they've got.' Then she thought of the photo on the fridge, of the man and the two girls, arms around each other, smiling, eyes screwed up against the sunshine.

'So what did you tell Rob?'

'I crashed at your place?'

Shazia shook her head, but it was mock disbelief, not refusal.

Ines thought she was the best. An angel.

Shazia said, 'And tonight?'

'Tonight?'

'What are you going to do?'

Ines looked at her friend, whose face was not quite in focus.

'At Bank. Tonight. Are you turning left or right?'

## 4

It had been a good week. Grief had kept its distance, slinking like a cowed dog in the shadows, never coming up too close. The twins hadn't mentioned their mother; there'd been no junk mail in her name. But this afternoon he'd left work early, knowing what would happen. The bank had written to them both: their fixed-rate mortgage deal – the deal she had arranged – was about to expire; if they did nothing the monthly payments would go up a hundred pounds or so. Another hundred pounds he didn't have, on top of all the other hundreds of pounds he didn't have now she wasn't here, wasn't working, wasn't being paid.

In the bank he sat at a wooden table in a frosted glass box while an adviser showed him leaflets, scribbling rings around figures with a ball-point pen. She said they could save him money, then gave him the forms and said to bring them in when he and his wife had both signed. And there it was, the black dog, snarling, saliva dripping from its teeth.

'I've been through this.'

'I'm sorry?'

'I've been through this with you – with this bank – a hundred times.'

'I don't understand, Mr Bridges. It's a joint mortgage; we need both your signatures.'

He found himself goading the dog on. 'I wish to God I could get my wife to sign the forms, but I can't. I can't.'

'I don't understand.'

'Watch my lips. I don't. Have. A wife.'

She said, 'I'm very sorry, Mr Bridges. If... there's been... some change in your circumstances...'

And he was off, roaring, now. 'Change? That's the problem, isn't it? Nothing changes. Five years. Five *years*. You know this. I'm not divorced. She's not dead. She's missing. If she were dead the insurance would pay the whole fucking mortgage and I wouldn't have to be here!'

The door to the glass box opened. Two men in suits stood in the corridor. The older one said, 'Is everything all right, Alice?'

He'd done what he could. He'd reported her disappearance to the police. She'd gone to work, he said. She'd left her phone, her keys and her insulin on the kitchen table, and just not come back. The policewoman made notes, and he said forgetting stuff wasn't that unusual. It wasn't the point. She had spare medicine at work. But no one had seen her since Thursday morning. The policewoman told him not to worry. Lots of people go missing: three quarters turn up within forty-eight hours. But it was already Saturday. He hadn't reported it on Friday because he thought she might have gone out after work and stayed over with a friend. She did that sometimes. The policewoman said ninety-nine percent turned up within a year. A year? A *year*? He'd thought she was going to say a week or two.

Later, when a year had passed and he'd put up posters and trawled the internet and a friend had made him a website so people could report they'd seen her; when he'd followed up the first few sightings and been to Hove and Middlesbrough and Cardiff with photos in his hand, and had caught himself about to buy a ticket to Denver, Colorado; when he'd had a serious conversation with someone at the support group about visiting a medium, even though he'd never, ever believed in all that crap; when, after all that, he read on one of the sites he still looked at that 210,000 people are reported missing in England and Wales every year, and he calculated that, even if ninety-nine percent turned up – one way or another, because he knew by now they didn't all turn up alive, or happy to be found – setting that aside, he worked out, even one percent still meant that more than two thousand people simply vanished – for ever – each and every year: about six a day, every day.

Had he done everything he could? Of course he hadn't. And if he had, what difference would it make?

Just a week ago, Aimee had said it would be her friend Rosie's birthday at the weekend and she was going to sleep over at Rosie's house, OK? And he had said it wasn't. It was not OK. He said you had to plan these things, you couldn't just up and disappear without talking to people first. Aimee said she *was* talking to him. She said: 'No wonder Mum walked out!' He knew it was a teenage ritual, but he still felt sick, winded. He felt as if he'd never breathe again. He felt the way he'd felt when Aimee, as a toddler, had waddled between parked cars out into the road and he'd watched, paralysed, as a taxi driver slammed his brakes and swerved and the wheels of his monstrous cab rolled over her feet. He shouted, at the toddler, at the teenager. He howled and raged and part of him watched, a small voice in the back of his head saying, *Is that the best that you can do?*

5

It took seven years, but when the sonographer somehow plucked twins from the blizzard of their early scans they were as happy and scared and excited as any parents could be. When it became clear that the twins were conjoined, they listened to the doctors and they read reports Rob printed off the internet and they knew that they would cope. They read about Chang and Eng Bunker, the 'Siamese Twins' who travelled with P.T. Barnum's Circus; about the Chalkhurst sisters, Mary and Elizabeth, born in Kent in the twelfth century and still commemorated in local cakes. They read about separation techniques and survival rates. The next time they saw the consultant he told them that, in a small number of cases – less than ten percent – one of the conjoined twins was smaller, less developed and parasitic on its larger sibling.

Ines said, 'Parasitic?'

'It will never mature and cannot survive independently.'

Rob said, '*She.*'

They agreed, just before the birth, that they had no choice. The parasitic twin would die, the doctors could say that at least. But about her host – her *sister*, Rob said – they were less secure: her life was bracketed around with percentages.

Rob said the percentages made no difference, and she agreed. Now that they had come this far, there was no choice.

6

When he got back from the bank he found a letter for Mrs Bridges - she rarely used her married name – from a catalogue company; on his laptop was an email from a man who'd seen her in Coalville, which turned out to be in Leicestershire. He opened the letter in case she'd made a purchase that might give him some kind of clue, at least tell him she had been alive.

It was a random mail-shot.

Nicole came into the kitchen. She stood behind his chair, laid her chin on his shoulder. She said she'd finished her homework, would he like her to cook dinner? He asked where Aimee was.

'Drum class, Dad. It's Thursday.'

Aimee came home just before six, and he caught a look between the girls that said what kind of day he'd had. She said, 'Hi, Dad. You're home early.'

Nicole said, 'He went to the bank.'

'And?'

Nicole shook her head.

Aimee said, 'Shit.'

He looked up, let it go.

Sometimes, she came back. He'd leave the door unlocked and sometimes, like tonight, when the girls were asleep and the house was quiet, he'd pour himself a whisky – even though he had work tomorrow – and take the tumbler and the bottle up to her study in the attic and scour the internet for signs, for any faint electromagnetic trace she might have left to prove she was alive. Or dead. No longer knowing which he wanted most. It was on nights like these that he would creep downstairs to bed at two or three a.m., and she would come home, late from some work do, and slip silently into bed beside him; he would wrap an arm around her waist and kiss the back of her neck. She would not be there in the morning. Sometimes he wondered what he would do if she ever were.

He put the letter back in its envelope. The gummed strip was sticky enough to re-seal. He turned it over, crossed out her name and wrote: *Not known at this address.*

7

That night, at Bank, she hugged and kissed Shazia goodbye. She took the escalator down, then down again. At the bottom, she turned left, or right – whichever – and caught the train that came. She would plough on, knowing it would make no difference now that she had come this far, knowing it would work itself out anyway.

# Isolation

MIZUKO AKAMATA WAS leading a horse into town when she tripped and the tether slipped through her fingers. The horse was a perfect bay mare that had been selected by Colonel Kichijuro himself – the first, her father hoped, of many that would be needed in Manchuria. Now she seemed to sense her final chance and took off across the fields, costing Mizuko's father an afternoon of unbearable humiliation as he chased the horse across his neighbours' land and up into the hills where the mist had not lifted.

A few weeks later, Mizuko stumbled again. She was carrying two wooden buckets of oats across a field to where the horses grazed, their heads down in the early morning light. The oats spilled into the mud. Her father cursed her stupidity, while her brother, Masato, helped her pick up the pale flakes. When their father set off back to the house, Masato mimicked him, rocking his shoulders and muttering nonsense sounds in a deep bass voice. Mizuko laughed. Masato grabbed a handful of oats and threw them in the air: they fell around her, clinging to hair and shoulders, like tainted snow.

In time she stumbled again and again. A dinner bowl fell from her hands and cracked on the floor. Her father screamed at her. She was useless. She was a mistake. Masato tried to intervene, but their father swatted him away. How dare he? How dare he contradict his father? Masato could not reply. They continued the meal in silence. When Mizuko carefully handed her brother his dinner bowl, he would not look up.

That night Mizuko lay on her mat, unable to sleep. She recalled the look in her father's eyes, examining it in her mind as she had not dared to do at the time, trying to remember when she had seen it before. A year ago, Masato had shouted back and punched his father in the stomach. Their father had easily won the fight that followed, but the look of something lost had stayed with him for days.

When her mother saw that Mizuko was still awake, she brought tea and asked what was wrong. Instead of saying, 'Nothing,' Mizuko sat up. She held out her hands towards her mother, palms down. She said, 'I can't feel my fingers, Mother. Or my feet.'

'What do you mean?'

Mizuko took the hot tea and poured it over her ankles. The liquid flowed over her skin and pooled on the floor. It was like watching a distant waterfall; one so far off you could not hear its roar or sense its weight.

'Mizuko!'

'Nothing,' said Mizuko. 'I feel nothing.'

Mizuko's mother patted her feet dry with a towel.

The doctor wrote in a small, soft notepad, forming the characters quickly, but with some care, then tore off the sheet and slipped it into an envelope.

'Give this to your father.'

Mizuko assumed it was a prescription, and wondered how her father would react. He was not rich – nobody who farmed on Hokkaido ever was – but neither was he poor. He sold the horses they raised to the Imperial Cavalry. But the doctor would have to be paid, and medicine might be expensive. She had no idea how much her illness might cost, how it might compare, say, to the value of a horse or an acre of potatoes. She had no idea what was wrong with her.

When her father read the note he seemed to shrink and become harder, tougher, like an almond that had been left too long uneaten. She had expected anger, but this concentrated stillness was far more frightening.

Mizuko's mother said, 'What is it? What's wrong with her?' When her husband did not reply, she took the note from his hands. Mizuko watched her mother's face turn pale, just like her father's.

'What is it?' Mizuko said.

'Go to bed, now, Mizuko. We will talk about it in the morning.'

When she awoke, neither her father nor Masato was in the house. They had gone into town, her mother said. Mizuko and her mother ate breakfast together, during which they were quiet, or talked about nothing that mattered. After breakfast Mizuko's mother handed her a small canvas bag.

'There's food here,' she said. 'A little money, and your dress.'

Mizuko said, 'I don't understand.'

Her mother handed her the doctor's note. 'You must go there.'

Mizuko took the note. It was not a prescription, but an address, with a long and complicated set of directions. She had no idea what it meant.

She said, 'What is it? How long must I stay?'

Her mother shook her head. Mizuko, now crying, stepped forward. Her mother backed away.

'Please. You must go now.'

Mizuko stepped forward more quickly and managed to throw her arms around her mother. She felt her mother's body stiffen, like a bird she had caught in her hands, then soften and become still, her heart beating fast and faint.

'Go. We must pray that it will not take long.'

Mizuko was already tall for her age. Her mother's face was pressed into her shoulder and Mizuko wondered if she had heard the same words that her mother had spoken.

The journey took two days. When she climbed down from the bus on the first evening, Mizuko was already further from home than she had ever been. She walked to a field at the edge of the small town, lay down behind a tree where she hoped no one would see her, and waited for sleep. In the morning she took a cart, using up most of the money her mother had given her; it would not be possible to return. The road they took was no more than a track. It was not marked on any map, the cart driver told her. When he would go no further, she followed the path on foot, obeying the doctor's directions, stumbling over rocks and into mud ruts. It was summer and the mud had dried. It must be the dust, she thought, that made her eyes itch so.

When she arrived, the gates were not locked. She walked through, towards two rows of low, white-painted wooden cabins.

'You are new.' The voice came from behind her.

She turned. An old man now stood between her and the gates. Where his eyes should have been, there were two black pits. His skin was grey; rutted and creased, like the ice-scraped lava on the mountainsides above her father's farm.

'Come here,' he said.

Reluctantly, Mizuko walked towards him. She stopped a couple of yards away.

'Closer.'

She took a tiny step forward, two steps. He raised both arms. With knotted hands like two fists of ginger, he scraped her face. Mizuko flinched.

He said again, 'You are new.'

She nodded, trying not to cry.

'And you can still see.'

She nodded again, although it was not a question.

He said, 'My name is Akira Fujisawa.' He paused, as if expecting her to recognise it. 'I will show you how things are here.'

He led her, his step sure, past the rows of cabins, to a hut set back on its own among the dark trees. The cabins were dormitories, Fujisawa explained. Women on the left, men on the right. That was where she would sleep, and eat. The hut was the medical director's office. He left her at the door.

'Goodbye, Akamata-joshi. We will meet again soon.' He smiled, cracking his pumice-stone face. His words, and the form of address he used, were respectful, but Mizuko could not be sure that he was not mocking her.

The director was a small man with round wire glasses and a smooth, plump face. He was sitting behind a large desk, and did not move when she entered. He called an assistant and told Mizuko to hand over her bag. The assistant pulled out her dress and dropped it on the floor. He emptied her purse into his hand and counted the remaining coins. He spoke a number to the director, who pulled open a drawer and took out a small bowl, from which he picked four smooth wooden discs. He pushed them across his desk towards her.

'We have our own currency here.'

Mizuko did not understand. The director shut his eyes briefly behind his glasses. 'Take off your clothes.'

Mizuko glanced at the assistant, appealing for help. The assistant said nothing.

'Here?'

The director said, 'Your things must be burned immediately.'

'Please.'

The director stood up. 'Immediately. You must understand, Akamata-san. You're not a girl any more. You are a leper.'

Mizuko bowed her head and shrugged off her pale cotton tunic.

*

Lauren lay back on the bed. Above her, a smoke detector's red eye blinked. Twenty floors below, Shinjuku district heaved and crawled with cars and bikes and people, millions of people. Lights flashed – Sony, Toyota, Starbucks; KFC and Toys'R'Us and Baby Gap. Money poured from hand to hand, a constant wash and suck like a turning tide, as salarymen and students shook themselves and rose, a foot taller than their grandparents, from the slumber of Japan's lost decade. In Lauren's double-glazed and air-conditioned room there was only silence. Then Gower was saying down the line, 'And this is worth a flight and three days out of Tokyo?' and she was saying: 'It's *the* story here right now.' She knew it was. And it was her story. She was the only European correspondent in Japan who knew the first thing about it. It was hers, by right.

The taxi driver at Sapporo airport spoke English. He would take her to the nearest town. He knew the road but was not prepared to drive her all the way.

'It's not contagious,' Lauren said. 'They have drugs.'

'I know that.' The driver managed to sound offended, as if she had insulted his intelligence. 'I just don't want to go there.'

So Lauren walked the last half mile alone, picking her way up the rutted, half-made road that climbed through dense forest, thankful that she had chosen to wear the trainers she had bought in Tokyo, thankful for the shade of the trees and the cool of early morning. Thankful too for the very tedium of the journey, the distance it would put between her and the others. It was here in the far north, in Hokkaido, that her story was to be found. Not in Kumamoto, where the court ruling had forced the prime minister to offer compensation – and, more shameful still, an apology – and where reporters squabbled like hyenas at the kill. When she rang the Ministry of Health, she told them she wasn't interested in the politics, in the scandal; she wanted the long view, the early days of forced isolation. The official at the Ministry spoke of the 'No Leprosy in Our Prefecture Movement' as if it were something that had happened in another country. Lauren said she knew anybody who'd been quarantined then would be very old, but she would still like to interview them if it was at all possible. The official hesitated. Particularly women, she said: those who had spent their lives in isolation. That was her story, she said. The official consulted his superior, then rang back, referring her to the director of a leprosarium in Hokkaido. A rising star, the official said. He would certainly be able to help. She had been grateful: now she hoped she had not been fobbed off with a provincial yes-man.

At the gate there was an intercom. She pushed the button and waited, practising her lines: 'I have an appointment with Dr Kasana. My name is Lauren Walker.' The two phrases had been culled from her guidebook. Whatever was said in response, she could keep repeating them until she was admitted. When a woman's voice fizzed through the intercom she repeated her lines. After a slight pause, the voice said, in English, 'Of course. Please wait.'

*

Mizuko was still naked when the assistant led her to a water tank outside one of the dormitories. He instructed her to wash thoroughly and then handed her a plain brown smock and trousers. When she was dressed he held out a sleeping mat. He led her into the last in the row of women's cabins and pointed to where she should place the mat. A couple of feet away, below a window, an old woman lay curled like a hare. She sat up and smiled and said, 'Welcome to purgatory.' The smile frightened Mizuko more than the words. The woman's face was long and sallow, with nothing Mizuko could recognise as eyes or a nose. It reminded her of a cow's skull she had once found in the fields near home, picked clean by crows.

'Do you believe in purgatory?' the woman said.

Mizuko said she didn't know.

'I'm a Catholic. I believe in heaven and hell.' The woman gestured around her. 'And purgatory.'

'Shut up,' the assistant said without much conviction, as he left. 'You'll scare her.'

The old woman patted the mat beside her. Mizuko did not move. The woman reached for her wrist and pulled her down to the floor. With her free hand she felt Mizuko's face. 'You are young.'

'I'm fourteen.'

The old woman said, 'Most of the men here are pigs. They say it's the drugs the doctor dishes out that make them so horny.' She pulled Mizuko closer. 'The women too, some of them. But it's all right. It was worse before Akira Fujisawa came.'

Mizuko said, 'The one I met? The old man?'

The woman clucked. 'Old? Nobody here is old. Fujisawa-kun is twenty-seven.' Before Fujisawa came, she said, there were no latrines. They did their business in the woods, in the fields, wherever they were, like animals. Fujisawa-kun sorted all that out. It was Fujisawa – not the director, not that useless pile of dung – who organised the digging parties. Fujisawa was a real man. A force of nature.

Mizuko's head span. Since leaving home she had thought of nothing but what was wrong with her and where she was going, and yet, it seemed, she had known nothing. At home, her father used the word leper to curse the neighbours when he was drunk. But this woman used it of herself. 'Lepers must not contaminate the purity of Japanese blood,' the woman said, sounding as if nothing could please her more. 'That is the law.' A huge grin split her striated face. 'We are an offence to the holy Emperor.' She laughed, a sound like metal scraping on metal.

Mizuko said, 'My father called me a mistake.'

'Yes, well,' the woman said, laughing more softly, now. 'Perhaps he would know.'

This time the laughter reminded Mizuko of her brother, of the day she had spilled the oats, and he had thrown them over her. 'My mother said to pray that it wouldn't last long.'

'It's only purgatory,' the woman said. 'It can't go on for ever.'

★

A middle-aged woman in pale green medical overalls opened the gate and led her past two rows of long, low, white-painted cabins to Dr Kasana's office. There were benches outside the cabins, though no one sat in them. Lauren asked where the patients were. The orderly shrugged. There were not many left, she said. Some were still sleeping; others would be in the fields. The leprosarium was a working farm, she said, although the patients were getting old and it was harder and harder to keep it going. They grew vegetables and oats; potatoes. And rice? Lauren wanted to know. Not rice, the woman said. It was far too cold and foggy here. It was not really Japan at all.

The office was wooden, like the cabins, but painted filing-cabinet grey, and set back amongst the dark green shade of overhanging trees.

Dr Kasana greeted Lauren warmly. He was proud, he said, that representatives of the international media were here to witness the dawn of a new era in Japan's treatment of its citizens with Hansen's disease.

His English was good, she said. American; perhaps a touch of East Coast? He did not hide his pleasure. A memento, he said, of the three years he had spent in a New England teaching hospital. Naturally, she thought: Hansen's. He would speak fluent euphemism.

He instructed the orderly to bring tea and then sat back behind his large, plain wooden desk. Lauren heard the familiar Microsoft ping of arriving email. Dr Kasana turned slightly to his computer screen. He waved a hand at it dismissively. 'It's nothing.' On the wall behind him Lauren could see two maps: one of the Japanese islands, showing Hokkaido far to the north, the other a map of the world; both were dotted with red and yellow pins. 'When I arrived here,' Dr Kasana said, 'there were no computers.'

'When was that?'

'Ten years ago, in 1991. The rest of the medical world had moved on, but there was no money for us. Now, as you can see, we have caught up.' He smiled again.

Ten years ago, Lauren knew, they still forced people into isolation here. She watched his face closely as she said, 'The Leprosy Prevention Law was still in operation then, wasn't it?'

Dr Kasana's eyes flicked towards the computer screen again, before returning to rest on Lauren. 'Have we begun the interview already, Ms Walker? Or are we simply getting to know one another?' It had only been a few minutes, but Lauren felt certain that she knew this man already.

★

That night Akira came to the last women's cabin. For a moment he stood in the doorway, listening. Then he said, 'Mizuko Akamata. Come with me.'

Mizuko pretended to be asleep. The old woman turned on her mat. 'Don't be afraid. It is Fujisawa-kun.' Still Mizuko did not move. 'Go with him, child. You are lucky it's him.'

He led her past the huts and between the trees. The bright stars were blotted by heavy foliage, and soon she could see nothing, not even the hard roots and dry, crackling leaves beneath her. It hurt, but not as much as she had imagined. At home she had watched Masato help her father with the horses. Fujisawa came to her hut regularly after that, always at nightfall.

One day the director's assistant called Mizuko from the field where she was digging potatoes. She had a visitor, he said, as if such a thing were a misdemeanour in itself. He says he is your brother. For weeks she had prayed that Masato would come. She had to tell him everything that had happened to her, to say it aloud. But now that he was here, she wondered if she had the courage.

Masato hugged her, then seemed to remember himself and stepped back, straightening his jacket. He seemed taller, somehow: stiffer. She wondered if he were growing up, or if it was her – her appearance – that had caused the change. The skin on her face was rougher, she knew. She asked after their father and mother. 'And you, brother? How are the wedding plans?'

He looked at the far corner of the field, where a man

was shooing crows off the potatoes they'd unearthed. 'I came to tell you that I'm going to Sendai.'

The name meant nothing to her.

'It's in the Miyagi prefecture, Tohoku region.'

Mizuko gasped softly. Tohoku meant 'north east', but it was a long way south of Hokkaido, on Honshu Island.

'Father has arranged through Colonel Kichijuro for me to attend the military academy. I'm going to train to be an officer.'

Mizuko looked into her brother's face; he turned away. She said, 'But what about your wedding?'

'Father brought it forward – because I'm going to Sendai, he says. But he knows that if the family hears about this...' He gestured at the fields around them, the cabins.

Mizuko waited, but the silence gathered around them. She said, 'Then you must not come again.'

'Of course I'll come. There'll be leave.'

Mizuko shook her head quickly. 'Don't worry, brother. I won't be here long.'

She watched him leave. Before he passed the cabins she had turned back towards the fields, back to her work. She bent to the earth and forced her fingers into the heavy soil. Now, she thought, she understood her mother's prayer. *Die soon;* that was what she'd said.

Soon after that Fujisawa stopped visiting her hut at night. 'There are new arrivals,' the old woman said. 'One of them is very pretty.' Mizuko cried then, but whether from relief or sorrow she did not know.

★

Dr Kasana said, 'You know there are colonies in Europe, too?'

If he expected her to be surprised, he was going to be disappointed. 'There's one,' said Lauren. 'In Romania. I've been there.'

'I've heard there are more.'

'Perhaps.' She'd heard the rumours, too, although mostly from the patients and staff at Tichilesti. There were others in Poland, maybe, or Bulgaria. 'In Romania,' she said, 'Ceausescu simply declared that leprosy did not exist.'

Dr Kasana smiled, 'Such is the gift of tyrants.'

Lauren thought: for years it hadn't existed here, either. Not for most people; that was the point of places like this. She said, 'I went there first in 1990 – about the time you started here, Dr Kasana. The medical director looked tired, more ill than some of his patients. I asked him why he took the job.'

Across the desk from her, Dr Kasana shifted in his chair. 'And what did he say?'

'He said the salary was sixty percent higher than he could get anywhere else.'

Dr Kasana nodded, as if to say: of course.

'I asked what would happen now that Ceausescu was gone. He said the patients were free to leave, but he didn't think they would. Most of them were very old. They had no money, no families. At Tichilesti, he said, they had medicines and somewhere to live. They had friends. They grew food on the farm. They had planted vines and were starting to make wine. A few had left, but most of them came back.'

It was all true – or, at least, it was what she had been told. She'd written up the piece and Gower had loved it. He said it captured perfectly the post-Communist dilemma.

Now Dr Kasana said, 'And is that what you told your readers?'

'I tried to say that they were people, but I'm not sure anybody understood. My editor said it sounded like a flea circus.'

'What is a flea circus?'

Lauren said, 'Gower – my editor – told me if you want to train fleas you put them in a cardboard box, like a shoebox? You put a lid on it. The fleas keep jumping up and hitting their heads on the lid. After a while they learn to jump just high enough not to hurt themselves. When you take the lid off, they keep on jumping just so high.'

Dr Kasana laughed. 'That's perfect,' he said.

But it wasn't what she'd meant to write at all.

After her article came out, though, it seemed as if every foreign correspondent east of Vienna had to visit Tichilesti, as if it were some rite of passage. Every few months a story would appear – in the *Times,* the *Independent,* or the *LA Times;* on the World Service or Radio Free Europe – expressing surprise at the 'discovery' of the 'last leper colony in Europe'. The lepers of Tichilesti were victims of communism, or of the new global capitalism. They had outlived their persecutors with the help of home brewed hooch. They were grateful recipients of European Union largesse. Sometimes they were lepers, sometimes they suffered from leprosy, and sometimes they had Hansen's disease.

She read that leprosy became curable in the 1940s; or the 30s, the 50s or perhaps the 1980s. Some details remained the same: the offer to shake hands as a test for new visitors; the empty eye sockets; the man who could stir hot porridge with his bare, fingerless hand; the burning of possessions and the confiscation of money; the emergence of an unofficial 'mayor' of the leper community; the fact that they were now free to leave, but didn't. Over the years, Lauren had watched these details float word-for-word – some of the words her own – in and out of articles around the world.

She wrote about isolation and forced labour and the brutality that occurs when people are invisible; about starvation and rape, about sterilisation and infanticide.

She read about flea circuses and wine.

She returned to Tichilesti herself, towards the end of the decade. The director she remembered had gone. His replacement said he was there because God sent him; he would stay as long as God required him to. She had not written up the interview.

'I heard at a conference that one can buy the wine they make.' Dr Kasana pointed at his computer again. 'On the internet. Is this true?'

'It is. St Lazarus red. About forty Romanian lei a bottle. Plus post and packing.'

Dr Kasana smiled. 'How many yen is that?'

Lauren said, 'I really couldn't recommend it.'

★

They told her the baby was born dead, but she did not believe them. She was sure she heard him cry when the nurses took him away. There was no doubt, however, when they showed her the body, even though her sight had begun to fade. My son, she thought. He looks like a skinned rabbit.

For her there was no war in China; for her Masato did not die in Burma on a British bayonet. For her the Americans never came; the Emperor never renounced his divinity. For her there was only the leprosarium, the farm, the small improvements Fujisawa forced the authorities to make. By the time the Showa died, in 1989, they had TV: most of the older patients were blind, but they listened to the soaps and, sometimes, to the news. To her own surprise, Mizuko cried.

'I was nine,' she said, 'when the old Emperor, Yoshihito, died. I remember my father coming home from town to tell the neighbours.'

'I was twenty-two,' said Akira Fujisawa. 'I had just found out. I thought if I could see the new Emperor, if I could touch him, I would be cured. But I also knew that couldn't happen. So I brought myself here.'

She stood and walked over to the chair beside his. She sat down slowly. She put out her hands and, for the first time in more than fifty years, she touched the corrugated skin of his face. She did not flinch.

★

This time, Lauren knew the story she had to write. It was an old story, the one Pascal told, but we had failed to hear for centuries now: we shall die alone.

'There is somebody you must meet.'

'Don't tell me,' Lauren said. 'It's your 'mayor'?'

For a moment, Dr Kasana looked puzzled. Then he said, 'Akira Fujisawa has lived here since 1926. He can tell you all you need to know about how things have changed.'

He led her to the TV room, where a tiny, ancient man sat watching news he could not see, with the sound turned down. When Dr Kasana introduced her, Akira Fujisawa held out a knotted hand. Lauren took it in hers. He pulled her close and felt for her face. She did not resist, or recoil. He smiled and welcomed her to his home.

There was a second chair pulled close to his, but it was empty: Mizuko Akamata had been dead more than a year.

# Aria
# with Different Variations

*Aria (1'53)*

TIM HOLDENBURY WAS a pianist: that is to say, he made a modest living – sufficient to rent a bed-sitting room on the margins of a gentrified corner of South London, and to meet his other, limited requirements (Bach CDs, surgical grade breathing masks, Venetian leather-bound music manuscript books, original Oxford marmalade, 0.45 millimetre interdental brushes, and food) – by teaching the mostly bored and disaffected offspring of his wealthier near-neighbours the rudiments of musical performance and theory, and by occasional performances of his own, the most regular and frequent of which took place on weekday evenings at a Chinese restaurant with gold wallpaper and a photographic cocktail menu on the fringes of the City.

*Variation 1 (0'45)*

If Tim had a hero, it was surely Glenn Gould, who was also a pianist, of course, although there the resemblance ended: for Tim knew Gould to have been an artist, a genius even (whatever some might say), but also knew himself to be neither.

*Variation 2 (0'37)*

And he was right: diners at the Peking Moon might, intermittently, raise meerkat heads, caught unawares by the music. But they never chose to listen, and the momentary effort was lost in the overheads of their meal.

*Variation 3 – Canone all' Unisuono (0'55)*
Each morning when the house was empty, Tim browsed the magazines and clothing catalogues on the post table in the hall. They belonged to Penny Briggan, who lived in the attic among sloping ceilings and dormer windows. Penny had red hair and green eyes; she loved detective novels and grew medicinal herbs on the windowsills.

*Variation 4 (0'29)*
From the age of eleven Tim had recorded a daily tally of press-ups and star-jumps in a diary that he kept locked in a metal box beneath his bed.

*Variation 5 (0'37)*
One morning in the hall, Tim lingered over a freckled Titian model in an emerald Land's End dress. Delicately, he excised the page. Later, he folded it twice and pushed it to the bottom of his bin.

*Variation 6 – Canone alla Seconda (0'34)*
A month later, Penny noticed all the missing pages. She knew it must be Tim: only he remained indoors in daytime. Online, she cross-checked the mutilated catalogues against their electronic versions, spotting common denominators.

*Variation 7 – al tempo di Giga (1'08)*
Then, one summer evening, while searching for her keys, she paused at the front door long enough to hear Tim's piano filter up from his basement room. The music was austere, the fragile melody exposed and bare. It stuttered as Tim re-worked a single bar over and over again, the differences too minute for Penny to hear. When finally he played the phrase through, she thought it perfect.

*Variation 8 (0'45)*
Of all Gould's recordings, Tim's favourites were the Goldberg Variations, of which he owned three: from 1955, 1959 and

1981 respectively. The first was Gould's audacious recording debut, in which Tim could hear all the confident swagger and unadorned emotionalism of music's own James Dean.

### Variation 9 – Canone alla Terza (0'38)

Tim realised that Penny knew, but she said nothing: surely that meant something? It was time to renew his exercise regime. He visited a gargantuan emporium offering all the accoutrements deemed necessary for a variety of unimagined sports.

### Variation 10 (0'43)

After much vacillation, Tim doffed his cotton facemask and sought assistance: he bought complicated running shoes and shiny, high-tech shorts. He had not known it was possible to employ high technology in the fabric of shorts; clearly, he had much to learn.

### Variation 11 (0'55)

He also purchased a portable tape player. The assistant was amused. MP3 was definitely the way to go, it seemed; but not for Tim, who felt sure that Gould would never have countenanced music that he could not touch. An original Walkman would help Tim to cultivate both his musical soul and his immaculate body.

### Variation 12 – Canone alla Quarta (0'56)

Settling into his new routine, Tim found that the park was a two minute run from his house: one minute fifty-three, to be precise, the exact length of the 1955 Aria, setting him up perfectly for the 'precipitous' (Gould's word) 1st Variation to propel him, heart pounding, up the long, steep hill which began his circuit.

### Variation 13 (2'11)

In time, Tim's run and the 1955 Variations melded perfectly in a doubling of form as he twice transcribed a figure of eight around the park, regulating his pace by the music's progress, aware, almost to the bar, that he was where he needed to be, the whole becoming familiar, then ingrained, subliminal as the liturgy: cresting the hill at the 5th Variation (and again, sweating freely, at the 21st); breaching the formal gardens at the 13th and 26th; passing, to the sprightly 12th, the exposed 25th, the couple ballroom dancing on the basketball court, briefly envying their companionship, before leaving the park and taking the road home, exulted, weary, *rallentando*, during the two minutes, ten seconds of the halting Aria da capo; the whole complete in thirty-eight minutes twenty-four.

### Variation 14 (0'59)

And the running, the routine, the discipline was not without effect: upon Tim's waist and musculature, which acquired unwonted definition; upon his teaching and playing, to which he returned each day with renewed freshness and application; and upon Penny Briggan, who at weekends watched him return and on weekdays listened out more often for the sound of his piano.

### Variation 15 – Canone alla Quinta (2'17)

Gould's second Goldberg was recorded live in 1959. Through interference and the sometimes muddy sound, Tim could already hear a more mature musician, confident in his own prowess, and in the music's ability to communicate – magisterial in the 4th, skittish as a young horse in the 5th – alongside an artist already growing impatient with his own reputation, peremptorily despatching the immense 25th Variation in just four minutes (more than two minutes faster than he had played it, without repeats, four years earlier); Tim reserved the 1959 for mornings when he felt sluggish, relying on its greater deliberation to give him an extra minute or so right up until the truncated 25th, knowing that he would have to make it back from pond to home two minutes faster than normal to keep within the recording's overall time.

# ARIA WITH DIFFERENT VARIATIONS

*Variation 16 – Ouverture (1'17)*
Tim felt stronger, more limber, *better.* Desire became engulfed, washed away in the pure endorphin flood of physical exertion, as the simple, fundamental bass propelled him onward, surging through the aching, piercing, stumbling treble lines, his sweat-sliding limbs pushed on by a driving heart and sucking lungs: it felt good, so good, oh God, it did him good, yes good: good to be home, to stop, to breathe, to shed his soiled clothes and scour his soul.

*Variation 17 (0'53)*
Earlier, when he saw the dancing couple, he had thought, each morning: I'd rather be you. Now, he clearly saw the woman was older and plainer, the man much poorer, than he had supposed; he knew he had no need for mere companionship, or love. In the communal hallway the catalogues went unmolested.

*Variation 18 – Canone alla Sexta (0'46)*
Penny noticed the change: rejection strengthened her resolve. She ordered all the clothes the missing models had worn; new outfits arrived daily and she donned each in turn, finding reasons to loiter on the doorstep, in the hall, copying the models' gangling, attenuated poses, and waited.

*Variation 19 (0'43)*
One Thursday, after successfully challenging himself to beat the '59, Tim realised, between his pupil's shrieking at her brother and her mother's casual enquiries into the whereabouts of her stash, that Chloe, seventeen and schooled at home, was good, that she could *play.*

*Variation 20 (0'48)*
That afternoon, returning home, he encountered Penny on the doorstep. If she appeared distracted, so did he, wondering if he might not, as he had always done with really gifted pupils, pass Chloe to a better teacher. Might he not, this time, teach the girl himself?

*Variation 21 – Canone alla Settima (1'42)*

For Tim the 1981 Goldberg was an uncomfortable masterwork, wilfully erratic in tempo, painfully slow in parts, sometimes executed with a harsh brutality. In it, Tim heard his hero, a year before he died, take the music that ran through him and pull it apart like a biologist dissecting a specimen, exposing the elemental and beautiful, the odd, diseased or merely redundant, but ultimately finding only that which he knew all along: that a butcher's shop may contain flesh and organs, bones and blood – everything, in short, one needs to make a pig – but yet nothing one could call a living creature.

*Variation 22 – alla breve (0'42)*

At the Peking Moon, when asked drunkenly, again, to play 'My Funny Valentine', he began instead a Schubert Impromptu. But as the manager blustered, Tim realised it didn't matter. He played 'My Funny Valentine' better than he ever had; his tips increased.

*Variation 23 (0'54)*

One Friday, Penny came to the restaurant, with a friend; she paused by the piano, affecting surprise, and introduced the friend; she explained (to the friend) what an exceptional musician Tim was, and asserted her own especial love of Bach; Tim, playing automatically, thought that Penny's green dress looked somehow familiar, although obviously new.

*Variation 24 – Canone all' Ottava (0'57)*

Afterwards, Penny stopped again by the piano to ask, hesitantly, if, perhaps, if he had an evening free, he might care for a drink, some supper, maybe, with her. He was free the following Saturday, which was Bonfire Night, he said; Penny said they could watch the fireworks over the rooftops from her dormer window, and blushed.

*Variation 25 – Adagio (6'28)*

In the 1981 Variations, Gould pauses after the very first note of the Aria – pauses so long that Tim, no matter how often he hears it, cannot help but think the pianist has died early – and pauses again, frequently but unpredictably, throwing Tim off his stride. The thing was hopeless: not just far too long; the timings were all to cock, leaving him anxious and disorientated. Climbing the hill for the second time to the '81's choppy, halting, agonized 15th (twice as long as the earlier versions) was just impossible. He could not use the '81 to lengthen his run. So, early in November, recalled by Penny's invitation to the purpose of all this, and scenting victory, Tim began instead to run twice a day, morning and evening, cancelling lessons to accommodate a final assault on the citadel of physical perfection. He detected progress he could not clearly articulate – a lengthening of his stride, perhaps? a greater fluency and economy of movement? – but which manifested itself indisputably in his accelerating performance. He found himself passing the basketball court during the pastoral calm of the 24th, crossing the bridge for the last time before the transcendent 28th, reaching home at the beginning, not the end, of the Aria da capo, knowing that he was ready, that now, if ever, was the time. Then, on Friday the 4th, in the early dark of a hastening winter evening, the music stopped dead, leaving him stranded by the rose gardens, stumbling, amputated, weeping with frustration at the truncated 13th Variation, and he realised, at long, long last that the tape player's batteries had died, not him, and it was revealed to him, somehow, all at once, that the batteries' death had not been sudden at all, but extravagantly protracted, the mechanism grinding inexorably towards entropy, the music getting slowly slower and slower: slower, not his running getting faster, not his body getting fitter, more limber, *better* – how could it have been so simple? – and he knew that nothing had changed and he had fooled himself, knew that he would never wrap a blanket around his own and Penny's naked bodies as they knelt-up, on her bed, and touched their foreheads to the cold glass to watch the night sky split and shatter into a million points of light. It would not happen.

### Variation 26 (0'52)

He didn't go to Penny's room the following night: he flossed brutally, then listened to the fireworks' crackle and the knocking at his door – tentative, angry, defeated – listened from his cold dark bed, lights extinguished, curtains drawn, duvet pulled over his head. Penny scaled the attic mountain, sloughed off another new dress.

### Variation 27 – Canone alla Nona (0'50)

In the morning, Tim convinced himself that he was free, but Penny Briggan lived in hope: she wrote a letter, with no scintilla of self-pity, asking why he had not come. Tim ignored it. He was no lover, not a musician either: a teacher, a dinner-cocktail pianist; he was redeemed.

### Variation 28 (1'11)

But Penny wrote again. Tim, thinking himself free, thinking to tease Penny for her delusions, set the letter to music, grinding out the words in Gould's own unlubricated singing style. Penny, standing at the front door in jeans, searching for her keys, heard him sing, 'Why won't you explain?', heard both the sickly, taunting melody and the deeper longing in the bass; she knocked at his door, and demanded piano lessons.

### Variation 29 (1'00)

Tim, a satirist by now, laughed 'Why not?' and dragged her to the piano, but found he couldn't teach, couldn't let her play without obtruding like some Pentateuchal God, until at last she elbowed him off the stool. He sat on the floor while a black leopard prowled the bass, sinuous, muscular, seizing his diaphragm and turning it inside out.

*Variation 30 – Quodlibet (0'48)*

The music transubstantiated into a blues he wouldn't know; but when Penny growled, 'Check all your razors and your guns,' it would have lifted hairs on the neck of Bessie Smith herself; and when she sang, 'We're gonna shim-sham-shimmy till the rising sun,' Tim knew exactly what she meant.

*Aria da capo (2'10)*

Tim Holdenbury is a pianist: that is to say, he plays more fluently, with greater awareness and control – more *musically* – than all but a tiny fraction of the population; but still, he knows, he does not play as well as the far smaller handful who can reasonably expect others to pay for the pleasure of listening to them, except as a form of entertainment secondary to their principal business of eating, drinking or praying. He still enjoys running, if only once or twice a week these days, accompanied by a broader range of music on the iPod Penny bought him, and which she helps him load. At home in the evenings, she still listens when he plays piano. Sometimes, when he plays Bach, she sings along; sometimes he does, too.

Total recording time: 38'24

# All Downhill from Here

1

'WHERE IS HE then?' The ancient captain stood at the head of the gangplank, running a thick digit down the manifest. I said you were a little late, that's all; you'd be there. He looked doubtful, peering up at the clouds. I felt the first fat drops, saw them spangling his beard. Couples squeezed past me, muttering, taking their rightful places.

I said, 'Come on, Cap. I'm blocking the way.'

'He's not here.'

'He'll be here. Besides…' I gave him my famous grin, the one supposed to melt hard hearts. 'Half a loaf, and all that.'

The truth was I didn't think you'd make it, even then. You'd be late. That's who you were. You were late the day we met; you'd missed the call and the pack had gone without you. When I came by you were in the stream. I thought you were after fish, but you didn't catch any. I watched while you dived, splashed, arced up and out and back in with a grace I'd never seen before. When finally you came back to land the water carved sleek runnels through your thick fur; when you shook yourself it sprayed drops so fine the air turned silver until the sun, glancing through the trees, caught it and pinned out a rainbow.

That was enough for me. I had never seen anything so beautiful. For a while it didn't matter that you were never where you were supposed to be when you were supposed to be there.

This was a time when winter disappeared and warm seas rose. In those days there were giants on the face of the Earth, tropical plants in the London basin; the Americas took their leave of Europe, of Antarctica; Africa stood alone, an island, watching the waters lapping ever higher. Things change, in the end. Nothing, given time, will be what it was.

At breakfast, then, I'd reminded you what day it was, how we hadn't much time, how we should stick together. But you wanted one last look at the forest. You might get us a brace of rodents for the journey, you said. I wasn't sure the captain would wear that, but you went anyway. When the siren sounded you were nowhere to be seen.

'Please, Captain.'

I wasn't about to drown because you'd got distracted by some fluttering passer-by.

The captain stepped aside. 'He'd better be here. We've got no space for passengers.'

Space *was* tight. Three hundred cubits by fifty by thirty cubits high sounds big to a carpenter, but there was the captain's wife, his three sons and *their* wives to fit in first: we were none of us fooled that we'd all get a berth. The old man did his best, walking from room to room, packing us tighter and tighter. I did my best, too, staying out of sight. If anyone asked I'd say I was pregnant, that one of me was more space-efficient than two of them. It shut them up for a while, until some clever monkey said, 'What if it's a girl?' Still, once we were underway, what could anybody do? They let me be. I wasn't food; I wasn't clean. After a couple of months, even the old man softened towards me. He began to seek me out, perhaps because I was the only one who was alone. The only other one, I should say, despite his wife and children.

'What are you going to do, Tasha?' he asked one day, after the rains had stopped, when there was still nothing to see.

I said I really hadn't thought about it.

'So think,' he said.

After a moment's pause – I didn't want to disappoint him – I said: 'What does anybody do? I'll grow old, I'll die. I don't need Ivan for that.'

I was only half right. I've grown old, older than I could

possibly have imagined. But I'm not dead.

Turns out the captain hadn't really thought it through, either.

2

When we finally struck rock the captain's wife screamed that he'd killed us all. But we stuck fast. The next few months, as the water slowly drained and the sea beneath us gradually became land, were not pleasant; the sons couldn't wait to get started, and when we finally got off the boat, the first thing they wanted was to kill something.

'An offering,' they said, looking at me.

'No,' said the captain.

'It makes sense, Dad.'

There was only one of me, after all.

The captain called me over, put his hand on my head.

'Not her,' he said. 'She's... unclean.'

So they picked and killed a few pairs you probably won't remember (and now no one else will, either). When they put the bodies on the fire, one of the sons said the smell was just like the old days.

After supper they stood and watched the sun sink over distant hills, turning the valleys and the plains below them orange, then purple. They sighed.

'Just like the old days.'

'Bags-I that bit!' said the youngest, pointing. 'From the bendy river to those hills over there.'

That was when I knew for sure that it had all begun again.

In the morning they packed their tents and started lining up the animals for the long trek down the mountain. The captain said he was staying put. 'I'm too old to start again.'

His wife straightened her back. 'You're not old.'

'I'm six hundred odd.'

'That's not *old*.'

They left, inching down the rocky slopes, the goats way out ahead, the hippos and giraffes struggling, the captain's wife clinging hard to one of the donkeys. The old man watched them go, his hand stroking my neck. Neither of us had said anything, but he seemed to know that I was staying, too.

He said, 'It's all downhill from here.'

'Yes,' I said. 'They'll be OK.'

3

They were OK: did well, by all accounts. The kids had kids; the kids' kids had more kids. There was always someone willing to bring food up to the man who'd saved them all, someone young enough to make the climb and curious enough to want to know what we did up here all day.

To which the old man would say: 'Think.'

Some of them imagined it was a riddle, but it was an honest response, at least as far as the captain was concerned. Thinking *was* what he mostly did, though after a century or so you might say it was more like brooding.

'Why me?' he'd say each evening, as the sun dropped towards the settlements of his offspring.

'Why not you?'

'I'm a sailor on a mountain, a fish out of water. Of all the men there used to be, why should I survive?'

I'd try to tease him out of it. 'Because you had the smarts to build a boat?'

Sometimes it would work, often it wouldn't. When it didn't, he'd say: 'Is that it?'

'You're a good man, Captain.'

'And my sons?'

'They're good kids.'

'And their wives? Their children?'

'They're all good kids,' I'd say, knowing that I'd lost.

The captain would shake his head. 'They're just people, Tasha.'

He'd hook his fingers through the collar he'd made, pulling me towards him.

'How much longer, Tasha? How much fucking longer?'

4

When he died I did my best to keep the vultures away. What else could I do? But the jackals got him in the end. They ate everything, even his face. I'd always said bringing jackals had been a mistake.

I watched the continents shift and the mountains rise and fall, and I waited for something new to happen.

Every now and then I dropped into the valley to scavenge food. I tried to keep myself to myself, but I couldn't help picking up scraps of news along the way. War and famine, mostly; some torture. Once in a while, a human interest story.

That's how I heard about the whale.

I knew at once that it was you, when you rose from the water, arced and splashed. When you opened your mouth and I saw that grin, those teeth. Who else could it be?

The story was you'd taken a wrong turn, come up river when you should have stayed at sea, that you were disorientated. Quite a crowd gathered, and stayed for days. There were TV crews, T-shirt stalls, burger vans, plastic wrappers everywhere. I hadn't eaten so much in years. I slipped behind the trucks, between the slick black cables like tangled anchor ropes, hiding in the diesel smell of dirty, chugging generators. I did my best to stay on the edge of things, but found myself pulled gradually closer to you.

At the riverbank, near an upturned rowing boat, I saw a woman in a pale blue jacket with a microphone. Every time she moved, her sharp heels punctured the mud like teeth in fresh liver. A man with a predatory camera perched on his shoulder clumped heavily around her, testing the sun's glare. Two more men stood between them and the water, not looking at each other.

The man with the camera said, 'OK. We can go again.'

The woman said, 'Professor James, we all learned in school that life began in the sea. But you believe that whales, like the one here today, descended from dogs that went back into the water. Is that right?'

She held out the microphone to the man on the left; the other man smiled, awaiting his turn..

The professor ignored him. 'Not quite, Kirsty. We know from the fossil record...' – another smile – 'that whales evolved from a hoofed land mammal, rather like a small wolf. It had a long, thick tail and sharp triangular teeth...'

'Dog. Wolf. It makes little difference,' said the other man.

I could have argued the point, but thought it best to stay out of sight, behind the boat, ready to run if the need arose.

The professor said, 'This animal returned to the sea sometime during the Eocene era, between fifty-five and thirty-four million years ago.'

'So,' said the woman, 'quite a margin of error there.'

You never paid much attention to time, did you, Ivan?

The interviewer turned to the second man; the camera followed her gaze. He wore a purple shirt buttoned all the way up, a flash of white at the neck. She said, 'Bishop Andrews, I understand that you dispute the professor's theory?'

He pulled himself up, rubbing his bald head, which had burned bright red in the sun. 'We do not.'

The woman's mouth opened but no words came out.

'God – Nature, if you will – refutes it for us. Professor James asks us to believe that a fish – he waved broadly out towards the spot where you'd last surfaced – 'can flop out onto land, turn into a monkey and grow up to be a... professor.'

You'd blown a spout of water twenty feet into the air.

'Well, let us suppose for a moment that the professor is right. What then? Then, he says, after all that time and all that evolutionary progress, a wolf might wander blithely back into the sea and revert into a fish.' He chuckled. 'Now I ask you:

if evolution works, it can surely only go one way?'

The professor looked out at the river, too, at the sunlight sliding off the greasy water. When he spoke, he sounded tired, irritated: 'Whales aren't fish. They're mammals. They have bones, vestigial rear legs that no longer connect to their spines: they used to walk on land.'

The woman said, 'Or perhaps they're *growing* legs?' She laughed at her own idea. 'Perhaps they're going to stomp up out of the river and attack us?' She looked straight into the camera. 'Mutant killer whales, people. You heard it here first.'

The professor sighed.

The man in the dog collar said, 'What I would like to ask the professor is: *why?*'

The professor shook his head. 'When a man of God asks why, he presupposes a purpose. A divine purpose.' He turned back to the woman. 'The bishop just wants to suffocate the rest of us with his comfortable stories and his imaginary friend.'

'But why would a wolf crawl back into the sea?'

'To find food, perhaps.'

The bishop beamed and said, 'Or to avoid a flood?'

The camera swung back to the interviewer, and the bishop turned away, towards the reeking portable toilets ranked along the high-water mark. Doing so, he missed the leap that you took then; the leap up higher than any you'd made before, up and out; the leap they later said you'd misjudged because your bearings or your sonar or something were all shot to hell; the leap that left you stranded in the tidal mud, barely noticing the splintered remains of a small wooden boat that pricked the foot-thick blubber of your belly.

The screams died away and the crowd thickened around you. You winked at me and said, 'Where've you been, kid?'

People tried to push past, the cameraman shoving hardest of all, but I pushed back, holding my ground. You loomed over me, impossibly big, unreal; your synthetic black-and-white skin glistened slickly against the dismal grey river, the muted pallor of human flesh and khaki clothes.

I said, 'You're late.' But the bones in your ears had fused and you had trouble hearing out of water.

Men with hoses and red uniforms pushed the rest of us aside. They dug channels, sprayed water on your back, waited for the tide.

This time you didn't move, not even when the waters rose around you.

When you died they cut you open. Some say they found a man with a purple shirt inside, that he was still alive. Miraculously, they say, his head was still sunburnt. I didn't see him, but I've no reason to doubt the story.

It's not going to stop now.

# The Truth

WE'RE TWO WEEKS into this, two weeks in a windowless room listening to the buzz of fluorescent lights, the scratch of solicitors' pens and the rounded vowels of both barristers, and I have yet to hear anyone say: 'Objection!' There is no shortage of cliché, however, and here it comes, from the mouth of my own legal representative, the one about truth I specifically asked him not to use, and he's used it anyway: 'Just because it is a truism doesn't mean it isn't true.' I don't think he takes kindly to advice from me. I'm just the defendant here; he's the one with the wig.

My barrister says I must not allow my mind to wander. There is a screen between me and the court but it is glass – or Perspex, perhaps – and the jury can see me. They will watch sometimes and if I am miles away they will think I am not taking this seriously. Juries do not like that, he says.

They don't like smiling either, he says: they want contrition, even in the innocent. I must not look as if this is all a joke to me. The charge is serious and my predicament real. He has made that very clear, along with the double-digit sentence I'll be facing if I don't do everything I can to help him help me.

I know that the clichés – *truisms are still true; just not who I am* – are simply the advocate's equivalent of the poet's wine-dark sea, of the blues singer's morning wake-up. The tongue flaps to mark the beat while the mind runs on ahead. I know all this. But the man stands between me and a decade in prison. I'd prefer it if his mind were nimbler.

He is not a young man.

Mr Simpkins, on the other hand, who represents the Crown, has a roll of puppy fat that peeps over the broad white ribbon he wears in place of a tie, and a ruddy glow in both his cheeks. His delivery is oddly mannered. He seems to pause for breath, or guidance, between syllables. Perhaps he believes it lends gravity to his words.

I try to appear engaged. I re-read the documents and scribble in the margins. I pause, looking up at the judge, with his half-moon reading glasses perched on the end of his nose as if he had deliberately dressed for the part; I gaze at the jury, who watch the parade with admirable patience, but who nonetheless doodle, shuffle their feet and discretely scratch their haemorrhoids; I catch an eye or two without smiling and then return to my notes, the very image of a concerned, *interested* defendant.

Before the trial my barrister naturally asked about my father, about my childhood. I said the facts were known, were not disputed and were doubtless in the files. I offered no more.

I didn't say that Sarah and I both did karate when we were kids. It was Sarah's idea, really, but Mum considered martial arts a little common for her daughter, and wouldn't let her go unless I went too, even though Sarah was older. Dad said he could see no harm in it. He probably said it would toughen us up a bit – especially me. That was the sort of thing he used to say, like 'spare the rod, spoil the child', 'put that down, it's not a toy' and 'a good servant but a bad master' (applied to most things from alcohol to guns to masturbation); the kind of thing, like my barrister's clichés, he used to say when he'd run out of actual things to say. He was a mixed-up soul: a Rotarian boat builder (yachts, not tankers) who voted for Wilson's white heat and would one day turn a Black Duck on himself and thus initiate the cycle of violence that has brought us here, to this courtroom. That last, of course, is in the files and is, no doubt, the version of the story Mr Simpkins will be working up. I see little to be gained from encouraging my defence to pursue the same path.

Before she left – left us to Dad, that is – Mum seemed to think we were re-living her own childhood, making do and mending so as not to embarrass less fortunate children, not rubbing their noses in our advantages, not letting their vowels rub off on us.

There is a rustle amongst the jurors, a flurry of interest. Mr Simpkins has mentioned sarin and some of them know what that is. But it was *ricin* that the so-called Al Qaeda cell in Wood Green was supposed to have been planning for the London Underground, not sarin. Sarin was Tokyo. Not that there ever was any ricin, but all the same: is that not grounds for an objection?

My barrister remains seated, and my eyes lose focus.

The Perspex is perhaps three-quarters of an inch thick and has a row of holes across it, like air holes in an upmarket rodent cage. They aren't really necessary because there's also a gap along the bottom where the screen doesn't quite meet the wooden wall of the dock and through which I can push notes to my solicitor. Also there's no lid, so it's not as if I couldn't breathe in here without them. They make me think of bullet holes drilled by someone with a machine gun and a very steady hand. Which (the idea of bullet holes) is interesting to me, because I now assume that the glass or Perspex screen is actually bullet-proof, an assumption that would not in all likelihood ever have occurred to me had it not been for the presence of these very holes that bullets probably couldn't make. The holes would also, of course, allow a bullet to penetrate the screen, if it were directed with sufficient skill, or luck, as to pass straight through without touching or being deflected by the sides. I think we can assume this was not what was in the mind of whoever designed this screen when he or she designed it. So what *are* the holes for? They strike me as some kind of destabilised signifier, alluding to and simultaneously undermining the possibility of gunshots and thereby bringing into question the purpose and function of the screen itself. Which, as I say, interests me.

I didn't tell my barrister that Sarah was nineteen and Dad had been dead about six weeks when she told me she was just glad that God is love.

We were in the kitchen at the time. We had not yet sold the house. She was standing by the kettle, waiting for it to boil.

I was appalled.

When I could speak, I said she'd lost a father figure. Did she really need another quite so soon?

Then she pitied me; and I had to leave the room.

My barrister had asked me about ricin before the trial, when we were going through the evidence. I said it was pretty useless, really. You can make it out of castor beans – like castor oil – and it's not that hard. You don't need much – about 500mg, which is a pellet the size of a pinhead – to kill a man. And there's no antidote. But the trouble is, you have to get it into the body first – as the Bulgarians did with Georgi Markov and their James Bond umbrella – and it's unstable. Frankly, I said, if you want to kill a lot of people, there are better things around.

I noticed that he had stopped taking notes and I wondered if he knew all this already.

When I was eight or ten or so I used to sit in the built-in wardrobe in Sarah's bedroom and shut the door. The wardrobe was deep and had a shelf where she kept underwear and t-shirts and netball gear. With the door shut and some socks pressed against the foot of the door it stayed dark enough for me not to be able to see anything, however long I gave my eyes to adjust. It was a good place to go when I wanted just to think. Sometimes I would fall asleep in there. For hours no one would know where I was.

One of the jurors, the one on the end of the front row, has handed the usher a piece of paper. This juror wore a suit on the first day and has been getting steadily scruffier ever since; I think he stopped shaving when we got into the second week. The usher carries the message to the judge, who reads it and nods.

In Tokyo, I told my barrister, sarin poisoned hundreds but – despite the fact that the authorities allowed one of the contaminated trains to run up and down its line *three times* before taking it out of service – it only killed twelve people. The problem was sarin's low vapour pressure. As it evaporates it disperses very widely, so a lot of people get a very small dose each. You can make it more effective by mixing the liquid with oils, I said – the way a perfumier makes scents that cling to a woman's wrists and neck for hours.

My barrister made a face and moved on to another point.

When the kettle had boiled and she'd made tea, Sarah told me she'd found God – not Buddha – in the *dojo*. In reality, she had found a man who called himself Elijah, who said he recognised her by the mark on her forehead, and who took everything she knew about God (from midnight mass and the poetry of Donne and Herbert) and turned it upside down. I had long since given up karate, but she urged me to return, to meet Elijah and her other new friends.

I declined.

She said, 'What are you afraid of?'

I didn't answer.

She asked if I was afraid of the whirlwind.

Mr Simpkins is trying to excite the jury with *The Anarchist Cookbook IV.* I especially like the 'IV'; like a bloated Hollywood franchise, it grows more otiose and incoherent with each accreted layer. I said something of the sort when the police first sat me down I don't know how many floors below the ground at Paddington Green and told me they had found the *Cookbook* on my hard drive. Along with all kinds of other crap, I said.

So I didn't deny that it was mine?

I was about to say no when I caught the look on the duty solicitor's face and turned it into 'No comment.' Now the Crown is talking a Detective Sergeant through the interview transcript, reading my lines in a flat voice while the detective plays himself, badly.

Later, when she was already living with Omega and was insisting that we sell the house, Sarah – Hagar – told me that the higher up you went the less sleep you got. Not because you were so busy or important, or not just that, but because the more you absorbed the discipline of Truth, the less sleep you would need. Three hours a night was not uncommon, she said. Immaculate Souls slept upright.

We're going through the contents of my hard drive now. Mr Simpkins seems to have something wrong with his right shoulder – a golfing injury, perhaps – and keeps rotating it before pushing back his gown and hooking a thumb behind the lapel of his chalk-striped suit. Then he leans forward, holding his forearm out stiffly and laying his fist upon the wall of files in front of him. He does this a lot, whether for emphasis or for the opportunity to scan his brief, I am not sure.

He is asking the witness – a Detective Constable from the High Tech Unit within the Counter Terrorism Command at Scotland Yard – whether the list of files found in the 'Omega' folder of the 'D' drive of my computer is the same as that set out in section 4 of the jury bundle.

It is.

Was it fair to say, then, that the content of the 'Omega' folder was the same as that reproduced in section 4, pages 1 to 322 of the jury bundle?

At which my barrister finally, pedantically and, in my opinion, quite unnecessarily, objects. Section 4 of the jury bundle, he points out, contains only screenshots of icons depicting the folders, sub-folders, sub-sub-folders and files contained within 'Omega'. The *contents* of the files would, if they were ever printed off, run not to a mere three hundred and twenty-two pages, but to approximately two hundred and fifty *thousand* pages. He rolls the words around his mouth to impress upon the jury the scale of the numbers involved: perhaps one hundred million words, he says. He pauses for effect, teasing the jury, then smiles, reassuring them that they will not be expected to read every word, although he will be giving them the flavour of a few.

Mr Simpkins acknowledges the interjection with a murmured, 'Just so.' The judge gives him a nod, and he continues to question his witness.

I made a hole in the wardrobe wall. I imagine that I wanted to see out, to spy on anyone who came into Sarah's room. Including, I suppose, Sarah and our father. The wall was only plasterboard and it took no more than twenty seconds with my penknife to pierce a hole big enough for me to see through. But now it wasn't dark in the wardrobe, because I'd let the light in and I'd ruined it. Sarah found me still in there, crying.

After an extended lunch the judge refers back to the note from the initially smart but now scruffy juror. The judge is a tall old bird with a nervous tic that makes the high back of his chair rock constantly: somewhere under that imposing bench there must be a knee beating a fast tattoo like an addict in a crack drought. Nonetheless, he speaks to the jury like a thoughtful brigadier putting his men at ease. He explains that one of their number has asked if we can be told why the police went to arrest the defendant in the first place. Which is a good question, I think. We've had whole days of policemen in bad suits describing the cupboards they searched and what they found, but nothing about why they turned up at my flat in the first place, at four-thirty in the morning, waving guns and screaming obscenities and pushing me to the floor, where I lay with my face in the carpet while they screamed some more.

No, the judge says, we can't. If the reason for my arrest had been relevant and admissible, it would have been presented in court; but it isn't.

When I was twelve and Sarah must have been thirteen we made napalm in the garage, which is actually very easy. It must have been a school holiday, I think, or a Sunday. Dad was upstairs, working. It can't have been that long after the stuff was being sprayed all over Vietnam and I don't know how we knew how to do it, but we did. We dissolved polystyrene packaging in petrol from the spare can Dad kept in the boot of the car. It made a sticky paste that burned like fury and stuck fast to anything it touched. We blasted an ants' nest in the garden. Then Sarah, I think it was, said: 'Let's make a bomb.'

I feel just a little sorry for this Detective Constable, who is marooned in the witness box again, saying 'yes' to each and every statement from the Crown. These are not questions, and nobody supposes that they are: the prosecution is simply entering evidence and the detective's role is merely instrumental.

Did the 'Omega' folder contain the four sub-folders ('History', 'Press', 'Theology', 'Tracts') listed at page 4/2?

Yes.

Did the 'Tracts' sub-folder contain the three sub-sub-folders ('Christian', 'Anti-Christian', 'Other') listed at page 4/154?

Yes.

And did the 'Other' sub-sub-folder contain the seven sub-sub-sub-folders ('Anarchist', 'Aum', 'Branch Davidian', 'Communist', 'Helter Skelter', 'Jihad' and 'Samsara') listed at page 4/247?

It did.

And did the 'Anarchist' sub-sub-sub-folder contain the document known as the *Anarchist Cookbook IV,* extracts of which are included in the jury bundle at divider 5?

Naturally, it did. We must assume that a detective can drag and drop, can burn a CD-ROM and print the contents, without materially cocking things up. The question is not *what* he found, I think, but what he *made* of what he found.

But it seems that isn't a question for the constable at all: Mr Simpkins tells the court that several more 'expert' witnesses will be called to talk us through the significance of my files. I catch groans from the jury box, and can't help thinking this a good sign. The judge hears the same involuntary sighs and asks if this, perhaps, is a suitable moment? Mr Simpkins agrees that it is, and another day ends in time for tea.

Eventually I am going to be called to the stand, where, if I am to avoid monstrously antagonising both judge and jury – and in all probability adding a charge of contempt to those I face already – I will have to begin by committing the common perjury and philosophical gaucherie of claiming the ability to tell the truth, the whole truth, and nothing but, with or without the assistance of the Almighty. After which false and inauspicious start, I will be asked to tell the court who I am and where I lived before my arrest and detention in October of last year. Simple enough, I suppose, but after that I will be asked what I *do*, a question I will find harder to answer adequately.

I have given this considerable thought. I will say that I am an intellectual. It is not a word the British care for, I know, but what else will do? *Kulturkritik* might equally apply, but is unlikely to meet with any more approval; and so much is lost in the translation. I will be asked – if only to forestall the same question arising in cross-examination – if I hold any academic position. I do not. Neither, I will add, did Goethe. (He was a lawyer.)

*Hagar the Horrible* was a cartoon about a hapless hairy Viking warrior that ran for years in, I think, the *Sun*, or possibly the *Mirror*. In Genesis Hagar is a girl, the handmaid of Abraham's wife, Sarah. When the Biblical Sarah fails to bear Abraham children, she offers him Hagar. He takes her up on it; Hagar gets pregnant; and then Sarah – whose idea this was in the first place – gets the hump. She is not terribly kind to the girl, who runs away to weep in the wilderness. But the angel of the Lord sends Hagar back to submit to her mistress and to bear Abraham a son, Ishmael.

The southern US city she moved to is an ugly place where, for most of the year, the air is thick and fat enough to spread on toast. It's essentially a vast puddle, a simmering swamp of oil and poverty, the downtown sky punctured by steel and glass monstrosities, where white-collar workers never have to sweat or meet the poor, because all the banks and energy company headquarters are connected by a network of subway tunnels. Tunnels for people: to walk and shop and eat and get to their car parks and their air-conditioned cars, like whales that swim for miles without breaching. I was there in January, when it was sixty degrees and the winter sun lit up the Library and the little park in front, and even though it was lunchtime there was not a soul to be seen: they were underground, some of them in lycra, carrying small weights and water bottles, power walking through the crush. It was without a doubt the very suburb of hell, and, for the first time, after all my research, I understood why Omega might have chosen it to welcome the Apocalypse.

When I say 'bomb' I'm probably overstating the case (although I doubt Mr Simpkins would agree). What we did was pick apart the shotgun cartridges Sarah had stockpiled. Dad had guns because he shot pheasant and duck, which was something people did then; people like our father. He had three: a pair of Browning Black Ducks that turned out to be worth ten grand (at 1980s prices) when he died, and a lighter twenty-bore he used for woodcock. They were licensed, but – this being long before you were supposed to install a separate safe – Dad kept the ammunition boxes in his study, stacked between old boat designs and the books about sailing; there were always a few loose cartridges on the desk or cluttering up the back of the drawers with the technical drawing gear and rusty bulldog clips and ballpoint pens that didn't work. It was easy enough for Sarah to pocket a couple here, a couple there. Dad never missed them.

The cartridges were cardboard then, and you could get your fingernail under the flaps where it was folded over, pick them open and pull out the wadding. Then you could separate the lead shot and the powder, like wheat from chaff. We half-filled a jam jar with powder, and topped it up to the brim with shot. I stabbed a hole in the lid with my penknife. We got a bit of rag and soaked it in the napalm left over from our ant Armageddon. We stuck it through the hole, down into the powder, and screwed the lid tight. Which is probably where we went wrong. Sarah made me light the fuse while she watched from behind the garden table that we'd tipped up to make a blast barrier. Being napalm, the fuse burned far too fast and even Sarah didn't have time to duck before a chunk of broken glass lodged itself in her forehead.

Years later, if she pushed her fringe aside, you could still see the cross-shaped scar. Years later still, she said God had laid His touch upon her.

When my barrister rehearsed me, I said that I had held academic positions, albeit of the most junior, hand-to-mouth variety.

He asked me when, and where.

Not recently, I admitted. By the nineties, the university environment had become increasingly intolerant of those whose talent was for *synthesis*, rather than for ever-more myopic specialism. The literature faculties knew a little of Derrida and maybe Walter Benjamin, but nothing of Herodotus or Lucretius; of Augustine or Averroes (Ibn Rashd, if you prefer); of Bacon or Swedenborg or Niels Bohr. The economists, mostly, knew some economics, but little philosophy; the philosophers generally knew less.

I understand, he said, not understanding. But what was your field?

And I said: I am polymathic. I am not this thing, or that thing; I am everything.

He nodded, and scribbled on his brief. He asked what I had published.

Hagar had children – three girls. They were with her in the tunnels. She said it was encouraged. To increase the number of the saved? I asked. Not only that, she said. It was to increase the discipline of the renunciates, to demonstrate that they were truly free. It is easy for the young and single, she said, to give up their attachments to this world. They are indestructible; money means nothing to them and they don't yet know that the people they love and care about will all – *all* – die. By the time renunciates became Clean Souls they were accustomed to a life that offered no attachments. For higher members, for those aspiring to become Immaculate, returning to the world to lead a normal life – to work, to marry and have children, while yet remaining free – was the ultimate test, the most difficult training of all.

My barrister does not in fact wear a wig, because he is not, in fact, a barrister. He is a solicitor-advocate – a solicitor who, as he has explained at some length to the jury, has attained the right to address the higher courts, and indeed to wear a wig if he so chose. However, the hair on his head (which I take to be his own) is pure white; his eyebrows are black and in danger of meeting in the middle. The effect, it occurs to me now, is rather like that of the holes in the Perspex screen – a wig-lessness that, despite being in reality natural, nonetheless draws attention to itself and appears more artificial than the curled perukes of the judge and the Crown, which it thus affects to parody.

Sarin is also what Hagar, her children – my nieces – and six other Omega Immaculate Souls released into the tunnels beneath their adopted home, killing themselves and forty-seven others, in the last days of the last millennium. What sarin does, when it evaporates and you breathe it in, is to make your eyes itch, and then your nose starts to run like the worst cold you ever had. Everything goes dark because your pupils shrink to pin heads and you sweat and you can't breathe: you breathe out but then can't get the air back in and it hits you like a wall. And if you go on long enough without getting pumped full of atropine sulphate and having most of your blood siphoned out and replaced, then you start to drool, and spasm and froth at the mouth until eventually you're asphyxiated by your own malfunctioning body and its uncontrolled secretions. So I would hardly cook up a batch in my kitchen, would I?

Mr Simpkins has invited yet another Detective Constable to the stand. This one holds the rather slim Bible they use here (is it, perhaps, only the New Testament? Do the stern injunctions of Leviticus and Deuteronomy have no place in a modern courtroom?). He swears without apparent thought to tell truth et cetera. He is broad and short and, to my eye, indistinguishable from his colleagues, and I cannot suppress the notion that there must have been an awful lot of overtime propping up all of this, and that the taxpayer would be unimpressed if he or she only knew.

The counsel for the prosecution asks him to tell the jury what, apart from my laptop and its contents, he and his colleagues found in my flat.

Books, the policeman says: thousands of them.

Of course he did. I look forward to my own cross-examination, when the presence of books will be offered as evidence of my guilt:

Have I read them all? Of course not. My library is a research tool, not a stamp collection. It contains far more that I *do not yet know* than information I have already absorbed into my work.

Had I *absorbed* the books on chemistry?

Some of them, yes.

The books on military hardware?

Some.

Those on violent, millennial cults? On Aum and the

Branch Davidians, for instance?

Yes, and on Zoroastra and Gnosticism and the Muggletonians.

(There will be a pause.)

It was not just books, though, was it, Mr Markwell, that were found in your library?

I imagine not.

You imagine not. Was there not also a map of the London Underground? A map where many of the stations – all key interchanges – were marked with a cross? And no ordinary cross at that, but the double cross particularly favoured by the Omega organisation?

I will say the crosses mark the places I have arranged to meet women – women I contacted through dating and escort agencies. One or two of the jurors will laugh, and try to disguise the sound. I will not react, not wishing to appear frivolous.

Mr Simpkins will ask why there is no record of any correspondence with such agencies – let alone such women – on my computer; and I will ask: would you want anyone to find that in *your* records?

But you would keep a guide to making explosives and poison gas, Mr Markwell? You would keep that right there in the 'Omega' folder of your laptop?

Indeed. Because it is nonsense. A joke.

(There, I will have said it and my own barrister will drop his head into his hands.)

A joke? Mr Simpkins will say. Do you consider blowing people up a *joke*, Mr Markwell? Are dead fathers and crippled mothers and little children being torn apart *jokes*?

That, of course, will not be what I say.

Is it a joke to gas forty-seven innocent people, Mr Markwell?

Fifty.

I beg your pardon?

Fifty innocent people. You're not counting my sister's girls. My nieces.

You do not consider your sister innocent, then?

Of course not.

Do you condemn what she did?

I do.

Do you condemn *her* for doing it? (He will not let me answer this before he plunges on.) Or is the *truth* not that you wanted to finish what she started? To show the world that you could do it better? That you could – in your own twisted terms – do it *right*?

I imagine that is how it will go.

But where is the evidence?

The *Anarchist Cookbook IV*?

I have been told to leave my defence in the hands of the defence. What, then, will *my* barrister (who is not a barrister) say to all this... *blather*?

He will say that the jury should know that there are many facts in this case that are not disputed. The laptop is mine, its contents mine. The castor bean plants (*ricinus communis*) are mine; the map of the London Underground – with its distinctive double-cross marks – is mine. My sister Sarah, also known as Hagar, was indeed a member of Omega; she died, along with her daughters, six more cult members and forty-seven others, in a poison gas attack in the subways of a southern US city on the afternoon of Friday, 31st December, 1999. He will say that years before, my father did indeed put both barrels of a very expensive shotgun in his mouth and blow his brains across my sister's bedroom while she screamed at him to give us all a break and do it then, just do it, and I watched silently from inside the wardrobe. None of this is disputed (which is not to say that it is true, or the whole truth). The question, my wig-less advocate will say, turning to the jury with a slight smile and his arms held wide in a gesture of submission, the question is what you choose to *make* of these undisputed facts.

He will, at my suggestion, introduce you to the principle of Occam's razor, which, in its popularised form, maintains that the simplest explanation of any observation, the one that least relies on further supposition, is the most likely to be true.

And what might be the simple explanation of our undisputed facts?

He will doubtless smile again as he reminds you that the burden of proof lies with the Crown. It is not his job to prove anything, but (and here he will pause for a little crowd-pleasing business), if he might, he would like to help his learned friend to see a simpler story, one that does not require us to believe in decades-old grievances and international conspiracies and goodness knows what else. He will say – and has advised me to say, although I will balk at the cliché, at the reductive simplification – that the man the Crown has presented to you is *just not who I am*.

And then the advocate for my defence will paint a different, simpler, picture: that of a lonely middle-aged man who lost a father at a vulnerable age and a much-loved sister in circumstances that were certainly criminal, but no less tragic for that. A fifty year-old man who has lived for three decades on the remnants of his father's fortune, a would-be academic who has never held a tenured post, a writer whose books have never been published – and never will. A man without friends; without a lover, without a wife. A man who kept castor bean plants because they are attractive and their leaves can be used as organic pesticide. A man whose reaction to his sister's death – collecting articles and facts and histories of the Omega cult, and of a ragbag of other weird, extreme and, yes, dangerous beliefs and organisations – was an entirely understandable attempt to make some sense of the tragedy he had lived through. If the search had become an obsession, was that not also understandable? It was sad, tragic, even, in its own way – the waste of an educated, agile mind – but it was not criminal, or even dangerous. You might not like the man, he will say. You might, even if you pity his circumstances, find him arrogant, incoherent, unsympathetic.

That is not the point.

Richard Anthony Markwell is not on trial for arrogance,

he will say – or for loneliness, for loopiness or the failure of his career. He is accused of possessing material likely to be of use in committing an act of terror; to find him guilty you must believe that he intended to so use that material. He is accused, in short, of terrorism.

And he is not a terrorist.

Something like that, I expect.

# Safe House

THERE'S A BOY Mary knows – a boy? a man? – she will play safe and say a young man she knows who takes the train she often catches home from work. She doesn't actually know him to speak to, but he follows her. Or she follows him; it depends on which of them leaves the station first. So – not to pre-judge the issue – one way or the other they walk in the same direction, up the hill. She turns right, through the dark patch where the street lamp's been out for months, then left. He turns right, then left. She turns again by the wall of Virginia creeper; most days he does the same. The streets where she lives make a ladder, a trellis laid against the hillside. She turns left past the school, goes straight on. Sometimes, like today, he must go straight on before turning, because there he is, face pale in the amber glow, approaching the next corner. He is wearing earphones, humming to a tune she cannot hear. He catches sight of her, looks away. She slows her pace, letting him get ahead, making sure that they don't have to walk side-by-side. He carries a canvas and leather bag strapped over one shoulder. It bounces awkwardly on his hip as he walks. It looks heavy and she has wondered before what it might contain: work files, books, a laptop, maybe? Or tools. It could be tools. She is less clear of the options here. Chisels? Trowels? Old-fashioned, unfamiliar words. Awls? What do people carry? He doesn't look as if he were coming from a building site. It's true that he is wearing heavy work boots, along with jeans and an olive drab coat that buttons up tight around his neck and gives nothing away, but the clothes are too clean, she thinks. But what does she know? He walks past her house, keeps going up the hill and she turns in at the gate, safe.

Except she isn't, because there by the gate she sees

something on the ground: a book, a notebook; plain black, held closed by a band of elastic stitched into the back cover. She bends down to pick it up and, doing so, she thinks she catches a glimpse of him looking back at her. By the time she straightens up he is facing forward, away from her; heading for home. She calls out, not loudly, and he does not seem to hear; certainly he does not react. She recalls that he wears earphones; it is probable that he has not heard her. She will not chase after him. She drops the notebook into her own bag while she unlocks the door.

She doesn't catch the same train every day. Sometimes she works late; sometimes she comes from meetings with her authors, or their agents, and travels back from a different direction. Some days he isn't there, on the train, either.

He looks about eighteen, she thinks. But she knows that she is not good at guessing the age of anyone much younger than herself. She doesn't think anyone is, really. There is a moment in novels – crime novels mostly, American ones especially, which really aren't her thing – a moment that always irritates her, where the hero, the detective, looks at someone, as he might look at her, and thinks: late forties, five-eight, black hair, a hundred and twenty pounds, good at crosswords. And she always thinks: how do you *know*?

The first time he followed her – or, at least, the first time she had noticed him following her – she had been scared. Each time she turned, he turned, his footsteps falling into a rhythm that matched hers. It could not be mere coincidence, surely? She had turned in at her gate, keys already in her hand – for speed, for self-defence – and quickly climbed the steps to the front door. She had turned the mortise lock and was struggling with the Yale when he walked straight past the gate, not looking her way. She slammed the door behind her and, before she could catch herself, called out: 'Nick!' Then she'd had to punch the code into the keypad before the alarm went off. After that she'd had supper to make and proofs to read.

The second time he followed her she'd been scared, too – though, strictly speaking, she had followed *him*, that time, because she slowed down so much he wound up well ahead of her. He was so far ahead by the time she reached home that she watched him safely from the gate. He kept going at the top of the hill, so perhaps he didn't live in her street after all, perhaps he cut through the park to the flats on the other side?

If he is eighteen, he could be still at school. She doesn't think he's that young.

She has a manuscript to read tonight – the memoir of a mid-list novelist with two good novels to his name (she had edited both). One had been shortlisted for a prize, but neither had sold more than a few hundred copies. The paperbacks had done better, but not much. Now, when her house is deciding whether to renew his contract, he has – against her own advice, but following that of his agent – written a memoir about his relationship with his abusive father. And the agent is threatening – *threatening!* – to take the book elsewhere. Mary likes the author. He flirts with her shamelessly, says she reminds him of a famous film star of the silent era. But that isn't why she likes him: the novels really were good, and she thinks he could do so much better. He just isn't really what her colleagues call a 'property'. She has had lunch today with his agent: a dreadful woman who not only tried to intimidate her, but insisted on a fashionable and unsatisfactory restaurant in which to do so. The lunch has left her feeling simultaneously queasy and hungry. She makes an omelette and a salad, and decides against a glass of wine. Maybe later, if she finishes the manuscript.

She works at the kitchen table, picking at the food with one hand, turning pages and pencilling margin notes with the other. A Haydn cello concerto rolls from the CD player Nick stuck to the kitchen wall with super glue when he couldn't get the screws to hold in the shitting soft plaster. The memoir is not bad. It might even have been shocking, had these things not ceased to shock. As it is, she finds the book not disappointing, exactly – she had not expected much – but depressing, even a little boring.

The telephone rings and she is happy to be interrupted, even when the call turns out to be from her mother, ringing to repeat the message she'd left earlier. Could Mary come for lunch on Sunday? It would just be her and Peter.

'Just come whenever, darling. This is your home.'

'It's *your* home, Mother.'

'You know what I mean.'

Mary knows. She has been told often enough.

After the call she checks the messages – her mother's is the only one – and makes coffee. She carries her plate over to the sink, putting off the moment when she has to return to the memoir. She goes up to the first floor bathroom, uses the toilet, checks for signs of the period that's due any time now. They have been getting a little erratic lately. She washes her hands, watching herself in the mirror. She re-applies her lipstick. It is ten o'clock; there is no one here to see; but she likes to do it anyway. She brushes her hair, wondering again if she is getting a bit old for the straight fringe cut just above her eyes, the sleek points that curl into her face just below her cheekbones.

Cleaning tennis shoes, her father called it. Doing anything to put off what you should be doing. She thinks it might have come from a Paul Gallico story, and has something to do with monkeys and Gibraltar. Perhaps she will track it down. Or it might have been Thurber, another of her father's favourites.

When at last she returns to the kitchen, the black notebook is sitting on the table by her keys and mobile phone. She must have put them all down together when she came in. She picks it up, turns it over in her hands. She slips her thumb under the elastic strip, unhooking it and hooking it back on without opening the covers. It could be a diary. It is private. She should not open it. She puts it down, pulls the manuscript towards her. She will return the notebook, unopened, the next time she sees the boy – the young man.

That's the decent thing to do. She is no longer scared of him.

The memoir reaches the point where the future novelist's loveless, brutal childhood so undermines his self-esteem that, in adolescence, he turns to drink and drugs and endless casual sex.

She stops reading. She has to, really. When Nick's liver failed the first time, he signed a contract that said he wouldn't drink again. He told *her* he wouldn't drink again.

She looks at the notebook. She recalls the young man's face, the sight of him looking back at her as she stooped to pick it up. The tableau had reminded her of something, and now it comes to her: he looked, she imagines, exactly as a medieval damsel might have looked, dropping a favour for a courtly admirer, then withdrawing, certain that she would follow, that chivalry demanded nothing less.

She turns on the news, turns it off. She drinks a glass of wine and goes to bed, the memoir unfinished, the notebook unopened on the kitchen table.

She does not sleep well that night. Nick comes to her in the early hours of the morning, to her bed. A sober, charming Nick who undresses her carefully, kisses her wrists and the still-soft skin on the insides of her arms, her thighs, her stomach, her breasts, and who, at the precise point when she reaches down to guide him inside her, vanishes. And none of this is new, either. Afterwards, she knows she will not sleep, that she might as well get up and finish the tasks that she has left undone.

It is dark in the basement kitchen, but she does not turn on the lights. She fills the kettle, sets it on its stand to boil. She crosses to the refrigerator for milk. When she opens it a pale glow illuminates the kitchen, and she sees the manuscript on the table and, behind it, Nick. Again.

But it is not Nick.

'You took my book.'

She screams and drops the milk; the impact bursts the plastic bottle and cold liquid spreads around her feet. It glows, opalescent in the half-light. By the time she looks up, he is gone.

She checks the alarm, marches from room to room, opening doors, opening cupboards, turning on the lights. She pushes at the spare bedroom door and it sticks fast. It feels as if someone is trying to push it back, to keep it closed. The room is at the top of the house, at the back, and she has not been in there for months; but, when the door finally opens, it is empty, nothing but books and manuscripts piled floor-to-ceiling, the way it always is.

She does not sleep. In the morning, when it grows late enough to go to work, she slips the notebook into her case, alongside the manuscript. She will see him when she gets off the train that evening, will give it back to him then. On the way in, she tries to skim ahead in the memoir, skipping the humorous twelve-step anecdotes, looking for the love of a good woman to pull the future novelist out of the gutter and push him down the road to recovery. When the woman turns up, Mary is surprised to find that she is not the novelist's wife, whom Mary had met at the launch of his first book (she hadn't made the second). The wife was short and blonde and nothing like the woman of the memoir (who is five-eight and slim, with black hair cut in a severe bob, who wears lipstick in the darker shades of red and looks, the novelist wrote, a lot like Louise Brooks). Mary skips to the final chapter: the memoir ends with the publication of the author's first novel, but she can see no mention of his wife.

Her day at work is not good, although she has had far worse. There is a meeting on positioning the following summer's beach reads to endure; easy letters of sincere regret to dictate to aspiring writers and – much harder – to fading novelists who found themselves dropped by their own houses. There is an urgent, chatty, patronising email from the ghastly agent pushing for Mary's thoughts on the memoir. This really is too much: they'd only met yesterday. She will ignore it until next week at least; it is Friday, after all.

Throughout it all, the notebook is in her bag. She cannot forget this, even when she is listening to her director, even when she is on the telephone chasing Production for proofs of a biography in serious danger of over-running the retailer's promotion window. It is in her bag. She could pull it out and read it before she gives it back this evening; he would be none the wiser.

It would contain nothing. A young man's journal. Shopping lists. Architectural sketches. Specialist plumbing joints to be sourced. Lecture notes. Dear God, poetry. The first draft of a novel. A novel. Even then, she should not read it uninvited; it is not done. Besides, she has more than enough manuscripts on her desk: why would she want to read another, one that has not even been submitted? She will not, does not, read it.

She spots him on the train, further down her carriage, standing pressed against the doors in a dense knot of commuters, earphones in his ears, a book in his hand. He has the front cover folded back, and she cannot make out the title, or the publisher. At their station he gets out first, propelled from the carriage by the press of bodies. She follows, her footsteps falling into time with his, not allowing him to get too far ahead. As they approach her house, she narrows the gap. When he passes her gate she calls out, louder than before, 'Excuse me.'

He stops, pulls the earphone from his right ear, reaches into his canvas bag with his other hand.

'Excuse me?' she repeats. She does not know how else to address him. She cannot say 'young man'. She is not old enough for that.

At last he turns and looks at her. She has the notebook in her hand. She holds it out towards him.

'Your notebook. You dropped it, yesterday.'

He looks at the book in her hand. He says, 'That's not my book.'

'But...'

He turns and continues up the hill, plugging the loose earphone back into his ear as he walks, the bag bouncing on his hip.

On Sunday she takes her usual train – the young man is not there – and then the underground to her mother's house. Should she tell the story, she wonders, while this Peter fixes drinks? If she does, her mother will ask what happened – has she read the notebook? – and she will have to admit that she has thrown it away unopened: 'I was just so cross,' she'll say. Her mother will seize the opportunity to criticise the house, and the neighbourhood, that Nick had dragged her to (without ever mentioning Nick directly).

'It's not *healthy,* darling, living there alone.' And Mary will have to change the subject.

From the pavement outside her mother's house she sees a man in a striped shirt with his back to a first floor window: this must be Peter. He has grey hair, precisely parted; she cannot see his cufflinks but is certain that they will be gold: miniature Monopoly racing cars, perhaps; or dogs. He turns, a glass in each hand. Her mother appears in the window beside him. He holds out a glass and she takes it. They look down into the street and Mary knows that they have seen her.

It will not be too late when she gets back home, she thinks. She pictures herself upending the bin on the kitchen floor, picking through the tea bags, the juice cartons and the wet cellophane until she finds it. She will sit at the kitchen table, reading, as she always reads, with a propelling pencil in her hand, filling the margins, correcting grammar, highlighting a point she thinks important in her small, tight script.

The book will be weathered, worked-over, each page filled, a palimpsest of ideas and scratched-out images, over-written with second and third thoughts. She will read late into the night, correcting, annotating each verso, re-hanging a carelessly-dangled participle, matching a group noun with its verb, delicately unpicking a knot of tangled syntax. At the office on Monday she will attend none of the meetings in her diary, answer none of the emails in her in-box. She will work on, correcting, improving, guiding, removing the redundant, bringing up the parts that really make it shine until, by the time she has to leave to catch the train, their train, it is finished; until, between them, they have achieved something really, really good. Something perfect.

She carries this thought up the steps as her mother opens the door.

That evening, Mary puts on the kettle, warms the pot, fetches milk. This is not cleaning tennis shoes, this is savouring the moment. At last, with the tea made and poured, she sits at the kitchen table, the notebook before her. She picks it up, turns it over once, twice. She holds it in her left hand, pushes her right thumb up under the elastic and unhooks it. The book opens: it is new, untouched, its pages clean and blank.

## About the Author

**Guy Ware** was born in Northampton and studied English at Oxford. While completing a D.Phil. on William Blake he lived and worked with homeless ex-offenders, before training as a public finance accountant. He has published stories in anthologies from Comma (*Brace*), Apis Books (*Tales of the Decongested; Desperate Remedies)* Route (*Ideas Above Our Station),* Earlyworks and Leaf Press. He lives with his family in London.